RUNNING OUT OF TIME

RUNNING OUT OF TIME

MARGARET PETERSON HADDIX

ALADDIN PAPERBACKS

First Aladdin Paperbacks edition, February 1997
Copyright © 1995 by Margaret Peterson Haddix

Aladdin Paperbacks
An imprint of Simon & Schuster
Children's Publishing Division
1230 Avenue of the Americas
New York, NY 10020

Also available in a Simon & Schuster Books for Young Readers edition.
Designed by Paul Zakris
The text of this book was set in 12-point American Garamond.
Printed and bound in the United States of America.

The Library of Congress has cataloged the hardcover edition as follows:

Haddix, Margaret Peterson
Running out of time / by Margaret Peterson Haddix.
p. cm.
Summary: When a diphtheria epidemic hits her 1840 village, thirteen-year-old Jessie discovers it is actually a 1996 tourist site under unseen observation by heartless scientists, and it's up to Jessie to escape the village and save the lives of the dying children.
ISBN 0-689-80084-3
[1. Mystery and detective stories. 2. Indiana—Fiction. 3. Diphtheria—Fiction.]
I. Title.
PZ7.H1164Ru 1995 [Fic]—dc20 95-8459

ISBN 0-689-83860-3

To Doug, and in memory of Myrtle Peterson

With thanks to Marilee Peterson,
Dr. K. W. Chan, and Creg Stockwell
for help with medical and pharmaceutical information.

ONE

The light woke Jessie, though it was just a glimmer downstairs. She eased out of bed, being careful not to disturb her sister Hannah.

"Ma?" Jessie whispered by the ladder down from the loft.

In a few moments, her mother's tired face appeared below, illuminated by a flickering candle.

"It's the Bentons," she said. "Caleb says both Sally and Betsy are sick."

Everybody called Jessie's mother "the midwife," but she did a lot more than deliver babies. In Clifton, anyone who got sick at night called on her. Most people, Jessie thought, seemed to wait until dark to get sick, so they wouldn't have to go to Dr. Fister. Dr. Fister always gave prescriptions like "Make a poultice of chokeberries and rub it on your neck three times a day." He made a real show of it. He used to slip a packet of pills under the table, too—pills that really worked. Anymore, though, he just gave the folk remedy. Jessie hadn't seen any of the pills in a long time.

"Can I come and help?" Jessie asked Ma.

"I don't want you catching anything. . . ."

Jessie gave her mother what Pa called "that pitiful please look," and she relented.

"All right. You can carry my bag. But I don't want you coming inside until I find out what Sally and Betsy have."

Jessie pulled her dress off the nail by her bed and yanked it over her head. Then she scrambled down the ladder and took her boots from beside the door. She was ready by the time Ma finished dressing. Grown women had to worry about clothing more than thirteen-year-old girls did. That was one reason Jessie was glad she wasn't entirely grown-up yet.

Ma unlatched the door and they slipped out into the warm April night.

"Hannah and the boys never even moved!" Jessie said.

Ma smiled.

"They could sleep through a blizzard. You're my light sleeper. You're always afraid you might miss something."

Jessie grinned. It did seem like an adventure being out in the middle of the night. The village looked spooky with only moonlight and the faint glow of Ma's lantern. Shadows flickered on the path and in the surrounding woods. The main buildings of Clifton loomed like hulking animals. Jessie shivered passing the three trees in the square that everyone said were haunted.

"Did Caleb go on home?" Jessie asked. Caleb Benton was

ten, but he was the biggest chicken in Clifton School. "I bet he was scared—"

"His ma didn't want him to wait," Ma said.

Jessie waited for Ma to say more, but she didn't. Usually when Jessie convinced Ma to let her go along on these night trips, Ma and Jessie talked all the way: about the symptoms Ma knew and how she planned to treat them, or about Jessie's schoolwork, or about just anything. But tonight Ma seemed barely aware that Jessie was with her. Ma stepped silently, her face shadowed. Jessie thought Ma might just be tired. This was the fourth night in a row she had been called out. Ma hadn't let Jessie go the other times.

They passed the school, the general store, and Dr. Fister's clapboard house. Jessie couldn't understand how the doctor could afford a clapboard house, when no one went to him. Jessie's pa was the blacksmith, and he was always busy. Yet Jessie's family still lived in the log cabin they'd built back in 1828, when they first came to Clifton. Jessie had hinted more than once that they needed a new house, now that there were six children. After all, she said, little Katie was soon going to outgrow the trundle bed that slipped under Ma and Pa's bed downstairs. Where was Katie going to sleep then?

Pa always answered that a new house was too expensive, with the whole country in a depression. He didn't seem to mind. Hannah whispered that Pa liked the log cabin too much to build a house.

Hannah was just a year older than Jessie, but she said she could remember when they built the cabin. All the men in the village helped lay the maple logs, one on top of another, and then the women filled the cracks with mud. Jessie had seen other cabins built—had helped, even—and thought Hannah might just be confused. Even Hannah couldn't remember before, when they'd lived in Pennsylvania. Jessie wished she could remember the trip out to Indiana, when she and Hannah and Ma and Pa had traveled down the Ohio River in a flatboat. Sometimes she could get Pa to tell about it. Ma never would.

"Be careful," Ma said as Jessie tripped over a root in the path.

"It's hard to see," Jessie said. The moon was behind a cloud now.

Ma nodded and moved the lantern closer to Jessie. They were almost to the Bentons' cabin.

"Do you think Sally and Betsy will be all right?" Jessie asked. Sally was prissy, kind of like Hannah, but Betsy was always fun to play with.

"I hope so," Ma said, in a way that made Jessie worry. A lot of children were sick: Jefferson Webster, Susan Seward, Abby and James Harlow. Jessie knew it wasn't just the usual spring chills and fevers. There were too many empty seats at school.

"Wait here," Ma said, pointing to a stump in front of the Bentons' cabin. She gave Jessie the lantern and knocked lightly on the door. It opened immediately. Jessie caught a glimpse of Mrs. Benton, crying. Mrs. Benton was a tall woman with rough hands. Jessie had never seen her cry.

Jessie went to the Bentons' oilpaper window, but she could see only shapes moving. The Ma shape seemed to be bent over the bed downstairs. They must have put Sally and Betsy in Mr. and Mrs. Benton's bed. That was serious.

The Bentons and Ma talked in such low voices Jessie couldn't hear anything. And she'd get in trouble if they knew she was trying to listen. She sat down on the stump, placing the lantern on the ground in front of her. She should put it out, to save the oil, but it was a comfort. Everyone said bears and wolves stayed away from fire. All sorts of rustling noises came from the woods beyond the Bentons' cabin.

Normally Jessie wasn't scared of wild animals. She was braver than anybody; she took more dangerous dares than the boys at school. But all this sickness and the way Ma was acting worried her. Jessie wished someone would explain what had happened to Dr. Fister's pills. Even when he'd had them, people pretended they didn't exist. But they always worked. Why weren't there pills for Betsy, Sally, and the others?

It was another mystery of Clifton, Jessie thought, like the haunted trees.

Once, when Jessie was little, she'd noticed a box at the top of one of the haunted trees. It was painted the same color as the branches, but it held a piece of glass that sometimes glinted in the sunlight. The box moved constantly, even when there wasn't a breeze. Jessie had been so curious that she started climbing the tree. She'd only gotten her right leg up on a branch when Mr. Seward ran out of his store and ordered her down. At first, Jessie thought it was funny to see the big man run. But she didn't laugh long. Mr. Seward spanked her, hard, and then Pa spanked her when she got home. Both of them shushed her whenever she tried to say something about the box.

After that, the box disappeared and was replaced by a

piece of glass in one of the limbs. Jessie never told anyone she saw it. But she would have loved to look at it up close.

The thing was, neither Mr. Seward nor Pa had seemed surprised when Jessie told them about the box. Did adults everywhere have so many secrets, or was it just in Clifton? Except when she was a baby, Jessie had never been any farther away from Clifton than a few miles up the hill to pick blackberries. So she had no way of knowing. Only, the adults in Clifton seemed to be acting more and more strangely lately. They'd confer in whispers, then pretend nothing was going on. Pa had told Jessie that everyone was worried about the depression, which started back in 1837 and didn't seem to have an end in sight.

Jessie could understand people being worried about that—Pa said even the state had gone bankrupt. But she still suspected the adults were whispering about something else. What could it be?

Sometimes Jessie wanted to be an adult right away, so she could learn all the secrets. And sometimes she never wanted to grow up.

Jessie giggled, thinking of the fight she'd had just that day with Hannah. Hannah said the only reason to grow up was to get married and have children.

"Who wants to cook and clean all day? I'm going to be a doctor," Jessie had said.

"There's no such thing as a woman doctor," Hannah said.

"I'll be the first, then!"

Hannah laughed at her, so Jessie teased her about being in love with Chester Seward. Was she ever mad about that! It was true, though. And Chester never even looked at Hannah.

Jessie had overheard Hannah ask Ma if she would be an old maid if she wasn't married by sixteen, like Mr. Seward said. Hannah could be so stupid. Jessie wouldn't care if she never got married.

"Jessie?"

Ma was out the Bentons' door now. Jessie stood and picked up the lantern.

"Can I help, Ma?"

"We need to go out to the woods to pick some, uh, herbs."

It made no sense—they had every herb imaginable dried and hanging from the rafters at home. But Ma had a strange look on her face that told Jessie not to ask questions. Behind her, Mr. Benton came out and nailed a paper sign to the door. It had one word that Jessie could barely make out in the light: QUARANTINE.

"What's a quarantine?" Jessie asked. It looked like the kind of word Mr. Smythe, the schoolmaster, would put on the eighth-grade spelling list. But Jessie had never seen it.

"It's a word to let people know there's a dangerous disease inside, so they should stay away," Ma said. "Mr. Benton's going to tell the Websters and the Harlows to put out signs, too."

"Not the Sewards?"

Ma shook her head and put her finger to her lips. Another secret.

Ma and Jessie walked into the woods in silence. They passed plenty of herbs, but Jessie decided not to ask what they were looking for. Ma was acting too strangely.

Finally they stopped beside a huge rock that Jessie and her friends had played King of the Mountain on, before it was forbidden. Ma bent down at the base of the rock. There was nothing but dirt there, but she motioned for Jessie to crouch, too.

Then, when Jessie had doubled over, her cheek pressed against the cold rock, Ma began to whisper.

"I may have to ask you to do something very dangerous," Ma said.

Jessie felt a chill.

"What?"

Ma shook her head impatiently.

"You can't ask questions now. We may be able to avoid it. The signs may work."

A thousand questions came to Jessie's mind, but she obediently pushed them away. Ma smiled, grimly.

"After school tomorrow, I want you to tell everyone you have to look for more herbs. Don't let anyone come with you. I'll meet you here as soon as it's dark."

"Why?" Jessie couldn't help asking.

"I'll tell you then. If I'm not here, everything's fine and you can just go home."

"But—"

"It's important that you do exactly what I say. And don't tell anyone."

None of it made sense, but Jessie nodded. Then Ma turned away. She picked a few leaves without even looking to see what they were.

TWO

"**W**ake *up*, sleepyhead!"

Jessie groaned. How could it be morning already? But Hannah was standing over the bed, all dressed, her brown hair neatly braided and wrapped around her head. Even in the uncertain light of the loft, Jessie could tell by her sister's red cheeks that Hannah had scrubbed her face hard enough for both of them.

"You're not going to have time for chores if you don't hurry up," Hannah said. "I don't know why some people need years of sleep."

Jessie started to answer that "some people" had done more interesting things than sleep all night, but then she stopped. No one was allowed to mention Ma's midnight rounds during the day. It was another secret, though everyone knew about it.

Jessie sat up and remembered that last night was doubly secret. What was the "something very dangerous" that Ma wanted her to do?

Jessie had done pretty much everything dangerous there was to do in Clifton, she thought, without being killed. On a dare, she'd walked a fallen oak tree across Crooked Creek last May when it was flooded. Everyone was sure she'd fall off and drown in the speeding water. But Ma wasn't supposed to know about that. Jessie had also talked Pa into letting her help him shoe Mr. Meders's wild horse once, and the horse had reared and kicked his hooves at her. But Pa had pushed her out of the way then. Jessie couldn't imagine either of her parents actually putting her in danger.

"Jessie—" Ma called from downstairs.

"Coming," Jessie said.

Hannah flashed her an "I told you so" look and disappeared down the ladder. Jessie thought about throwing her brush at Hannah, but didn't want to take the time to pick it up. And she would get in trouble. Hannah would see to it.

Jessie got out of bed and pulled her dress on, no more carefully than she had the night before. The dress was a threadbare woolen that had originally been Ma's; it was cut down for Hannah and then passed on to Jessie when Hannah became too stout. Jessie didn't think it was fair that she still had to wear Hannah's old clothes. Jessie was an inch taller. It wasn't her fault Hannah was fatter. But people in Clifton didn't care about a girl's ankle showing a little. She'd heard Ma and the other women say it was a scandalous thing back East, but on the frontier people had other things to worry about.

Wondering whether she'd ever have a chance to see the East, Jessie began her daily battle with her hair. It was dark and coarse and uncontrollable. Jessie braided it as tightly as she could, knowing wisps of hair would begin freeing themselves as soon as she finished.

Finally ready, Jessie climbed downstairs and started taking the family's chamber pots out to the outhouse. She hated that chore, but it was her turn. Two of her brothers, Nathan and Bartholomew, were helping Pa feed the cattle, pigs, chickens, and horses. Andrew, who was just two years younger than Jessie, carried wood toward Pa's blacksmith shop. Hannah and Katie, the youngest, helped Ma with breakfast.

Jessie stopped at the well to wash her hands. Pa, heading from the barn to the forge, stepped behind her.

"Morning, Jessica. Did milady sleep well?"

It was his joke, to call his daughters "milady," even though he didn't believe in royalty. Jessie had heard Mrs. Seward say once that, for a Jacksonian Democrat, Joseph Keyser certainly put on airs.

"Yes, Pa," Jessie said. She looked at him closely, trying to figure out if he knew about the "something very dangerous" that Ma wanted.

"What's wrong? Did I forget to shave?" Pa made a show of trying to look down at his chin. Jessie decided he didn't know anything about Ma's plans. That scared her, but she clowned an answer.

"I think you missed a patch right there—" Jessie said, pointing at a spot on his right cheek and bringing her hand up suddenly to splash water on his face.

Pa laughed and splashed her back.

"Pa! I don't want to be soaking wet at school!" Jessie protested.

"You started it!"

Jessie dried her hands on her apron as Pa, laughing, went on to the smithy. Jessie had heard Ma complain that Pa acted worse than the little boys sometimes. With his curly brown hair and laughing eyes, he looked a lot like Nathan. Jessie knew he was actually thirty-five, because it said in the family Bible, "Joseph Andrew Keyser, born May 18, 1804, Philadelphia, Pennsylvania." Ma was three years younger, but she acted older. The circuit rider minister, Reverend Holloway, always preached that wives were supposed to be obedient to their husbands. It didn't seem to work that way at Jessie's house. Oh, Ma pretended to be obedient, but she was really in charge.

Only, Pa usually knew what she was planning.

Jessie walked slowly back to the house, stumped about what Ma might want her to do. Usually Jessie could find some answer to any question at school, even when she wasn't entirely sure. But she couldn't figure out anything now. In the sunny yard, Jessie almost wondered if she'd imagined going to the King of the Mountain rock. Had she dreamed it? But no—when she stepped in the cabin door, she saw the wilted leaves Ma had picked on their way out of the woods.

"No dawdling, now," Ma said as everyone converged at the table. Jessie could smell the salt ham from across the room. There were also eggs, biscuits, gravy, back bacon, apple pie, and mush.

The light from the fire glowed behind the table. The cabin was dim otherwise, because the oilpaper windows were so thick. Often Jessie wished for glass windows like Dr. Fister's, but today the dimness seemed cozy. Across from the door, the ornate mirror on the back wall reflected little light. Even if it was one of the few heirlooms brought from Pennsylvania, Jessie had never liked the mirror. Maybe she'd been yelled at to stay away from it too many times when she was younger. But she'd been told just as often to be careful around the framed picture of Andrew Jackson and the tacked-up map of the United States, which hung on either side of the cabin door. And she had always thought the map and the picture looked downright friendly.

Pa began his prayer. As always, it was long, and Jessie wasn't the only one to open one eye and peek at the food.

"We implore you, Lord, to keep our village and family safe from any sickness abroad in the land," Pa said. Jessie glanced up, but Pa's face wasn't any different from when he prayed for the wisdom of the government.

Jessie caught a stern glance from Ma and closed her eyes again until the "Amen."

THREE

Mr. Smythe had asked the question twice, and Jessie still hadn't heard it.

"The presidents," Mary Ruddle hissed. "Recite the presidents."

Jessie nodded gratefully and stood up.

"George Washington," she began. "Elected in 1789 and served two terms. Father of our country. Led the military in the Revolutionary War. . . ."

She zipped through the rest—Adams, Jefferson, Madison, Monroe, J. Q. Adams, Jackson, and the current president, Van Buren—without thinking about them. Sometimes she liked to mention extra details, like her father's admiration for Andrew Jackson, even though it got her in trouble. But this time she did the list straight. She didn't understand why the others, especially Hannah, thought this recitation difficult.

Portraits of George Washington and Martin Van Buren hung on the wall over Mr. Smythe's desk, so it would be impossible to forget either of them. There weren't that many presidents in between. Hannah's problem was that she spent too much time craning her neck to see into the mirror that hung beside the eighth graders' desks. Jessie had never understood what it was doing there, unless Mr. Smythe wanted to torture vain students like Hannah.

"And the next presidential election—" Mr. Smythe prompted.

"This year. November 1840," Jessie said automatically. Mr. Smythe always wanted his students to say what year it was. Jessie thought that was strange. Didn't everyone know?

"Good," Mr. Smythe said, and turned his attention to third-grade reading. Jessie waited until he wasn't looking and made a face. She didn't like Mr. Smythe. He had hairs growing out of his nose and a way of looking at students as though he knew something they didn't. Jessie couldn't believe he knew as much as the students, because he always had to check their work with his books. Just the day before, he'd forgotten the year that Miles Clifton came up from Kentucky to found the village. And he threatened to get out the whip when the sixth graders tried to tell him the right answer.

"Did anyone ask you?" he'd screamed. And when all the other students looked up to watch him yell, he began fuming, "Am I talking to you? Everyone has to stay after school!"

Jessie hoped he wouldn't make them stay late today. She sat down and saw that her friend Mary had written, "What's wrong?" on her slate.

"Nothing. Just daydreaming," Jessie wrote back. But then she felt bad about not letting her best friend in on something. "Did you see Sally and Betsy are sick, too?" she wrote.

Mary grimaced and nodded. Jessie looked around to count the empty benches. Nine pupils were missing between Katie's first-grade row and the seventh- and eighth-grade row where Jessie, Hannah, Mary, Chester Seward, and Richard Dunlap sat.

"Back row, are you doing your spelling words?" Mr. Smythe asked.

"Yes, Mr. Smythe," Hannah said. She was the only one, since Chester and Richard were drawing dirty pictures.

Jessie bent over her slate and wrote "independence" five times. She couldn't wait for school to get out.

But when Mr. Smythe finally dismissed everyone, Jessie held herself back from the rush for the door.

"Want to come home with me? Pa gave me some extra clay," Mary said. Her father was the potter, and when he was feeling generous he let his children play in his workshop. He once helped Mary and Jessie make a clay doll for Jessie's sister Katie.

"No thanks. I've got to pick some herbs for Ma," Jessie remembered to say.

She was walking out behind Mary when she noticed Katie still sitting in the front row.

"My insides don't feel good," Katie said.

Jessie stooped beside her and felt her sister's forehead, as she had seen Ma do with sick people. Katie's face was burning up, but the little girl shivered so hard that her teeth clattered.

"What hurts?" Jessie asked gently.

Katie pointed to her throat. She looked like she was going to cry, but she sneezed instead.

"Here." Jessie handed Katie her handkerchief. Katie blew her nose, loud for such a little girl, and began coughing.

"Can you walk home?" Jessie asked Katie.

"No," Katie whispered. Her eyes filled with tears.

Jessie rubbed Katie's eyes with the handkerchief's clean end.

"That's all right," Jessie said. "I'll carry you, just like when you were really little."

Crying, Katie climbed onto Jessie's back. It was awkward to carry Katie, both their lunch pails, and all their books. Jessie wished Mr. Smythe were a nicer man, and would come help them. But he was watching poor Caleb Benton erase the blackboards, as if waiting for Caleb to make a mistake.

"Don't worry. You'll be okay," Jessie said softly, so Mr. Smythe couldn't hear her. She didn't want to be punished. "Okay" was a bad word no one was supposed to say, but Jessie liked it. Sometimes she wondered if it was forbidden because it had a secret power to make things okay. If that was true, Jessie wanted that power now. She wasn't sure Katie would be okay. Betsy Benton had said she had a sore throat yesterday, too. And now she was so sick even Ma looked worried.

"Comfortable?" Jessie asked as she walked unevenly out the schoolhouse door.

Katie just sniffled, her face buried in Jessie's hair.

"You'll be okay," Jessie repeated, so quietly that maybe even Katie didn't hear. She didn't answer, only moaned when

Jessie stumbled and jolted her. As they lurched past the Websters' house, Jessie saw there was no quarantine sign on the door. Was that good or bad?

Although she stumbled a few more times, Jessie finally made it to the door of the Keyser cabin.

"Hello? Ma?" she called.

No one was home. Jessie's brothers were all out in the forge helping Pa, and Jessie remembered that Hannah had planned to stop off at Seward's store and look at some fabric she wanted but would never be able to afford. Ma must be at one of the neighbors'—which was strange. Usually at this time of day, Ma was in the cabin fixing supper. The fire was banked on a Dutch oven full of some kind of food, but there was no other sign that Ma had been in the cabin since morning.

"Here, we'll get you to bed. Then you'll be fine," Jessie told Katie with false confidence. "Doesn't that feel better?"

Katie's face was almost as pale as her bedding.

"Thirsty," she murmured.

Jessie got her a drink and waited until Katie fell asleep. It didn't seem right to leave Katie, but Ma had acted like it was important to meet her in the woods. Jessie stopped at Pa's blacksmith shop on her way.

"Can you tell Ma that Katie's sick?" Jessie asked Andrew, who was sorting scrap metal while Pa worked at the forge.

"Why can't you?"

Andrew was Jessie's favorite brother, but he could be a horrible pain.

"Ma wanted me to pick some herbs, and I don't want to go in the dark," Jessie explained.

"Chicken?" Andrew taunted.

"Of course not. I just want to be able to see."

Andrew shrugged, which Jessie took to mean that he would tell Ma about Katie. He waited until she had walked down the road before he yelled after her, "Sure you're not going out to meet some boy?"

"Shut up!" Jessie shouted. Then she ran, hoping Pa hadn't heard her.

"Shut up" was like "okay," another bad word no one was allowed to use. They were even worse than taking the Lord's name in vain. Jessie could never understand why. She could see that God might be offended at being used as a common curse, something she'd heard only a few men do when they appeared very, very mad. But even though Jessie pretended "okay" had special powers, she knew it wasn't black magic or anything. And "shut up" was maybe a little rude, but . . . Jessie knew it was no use trying to figure it out. This was another secret.

Jessie stopped running only when she reached the woods. With all the branches blocking the sun, it was always a little dusky and hard to see in there. She knew from school that the woods went on and on, clear to the Mississippi River, with only a few settlements like Clifton carved out in their midst. She kind of liked that, even though she'd heard some grown-ups talk about being afraid of the woods. She guessed it was because there were still dangerous Indians about when they came out from the East. But the Indians had all moved farther west now.

Jessie remembered the stories about the battles of Fallen Timbers and Tippecanoe and shivered. It didn't seem fair.

The Indians had been here first. But Mr. Smythe had threatened to spank her for saying that in school.

Jessie sat down on a log, thinking it would never be truly dark. Since she was here, she might as well pick herbs. She turned around to pull bark from a witch hazel tree.

And then Ma was standing beside her.

"You shouldn't let people sneak up on you like that," Ma said. It seemed like a joke, but Ma's voice held an edge.

"It's just you, Ma," Jessie said. She waited for Ma to smile, but Ma didn't. "Where were you? What's the dangerous thing I have to do? Is Katie—"

"Shh." Ma looked around, guardedly, then placed her lamp and medicine bag on the ground. She bent beside the rock as she had the night before. Jessie moved into the same pose.

"I think we're safe, but we'll have to whisper," Ma said. "I'll answer all your questions, but it's going to take a while. I did see Katie—"

"Does she have the same sickness as Sally and Betsy?"

Ma looked away, as though she was too sad to look at Jessie.

"I'm afraid she does. It's a disease called diphtheria."

It scared Jessie that Ma sounded so solemn. Jessie thought about her towheaded little sister, who was only six but always tried to do what "the big girls" did.

"Is she going to be all right?" Jessie asked. "Are Sally and Betsy and the others—"

"That depends," Ma said. "I have a lot to tell you."

Ma stopped. A strong wind rustled the leaves of all the trees around them. Jessie shuddered. But maybe that wasn't just because of the wind.

"I never wanted to tell you like this," Ma said. "Jessie, I don't know how you're going to react—"

"To what?" Jessie asked impatiently. Ma's voice frightened her.

Ma held her finger to her lips.

"Be still a minute," she said. "I'm trying to think. How do I tell after all these years? It's so complicated. . . ."

Jessie waited, not used to seeing Ma so puzzled and worried. Finally Ma looked back at Jessie.

"We've been in Clifton for twelve years now, right? Remember how Pa always told you we came here because there was more opportunity than back in Pennsylvania?"

Jessie nodded.

"Well, that's true, but not in the way we led you to believe. Clifton isn't an ordinary village. It's a historical preserve."

"What's that?" Jessie's voice shook a little.

Ma's gaze was steady.

"Here, everything's like it was in the 1800s," Ma said slowly. "Outside, it's"—Ma seemed to be counting in her mind—"Outside, it's 1996."

FOUR

For a long moment, Jessie couldn't say anything. How could it be 1996? Jessie's mind felt jumbled. If it wasn't 1840, last year wasn't 1839, and—

"Jessie?" Ma said. "Are you listening?"

"I'm trying to," Jessie said.

"Pa and I always wondered if we were being fair to you children. At least—I always wondered. Many times I wanted to tell, especially you and Andrew. But it got so it was safer not to."

"Why?"

Ma frowned.

"I don't understand everything myself. I know what Miles Clifton said in the beginning, but I can't believe it anymore. How can I explain what I don't know?"

Jessie had never seen her mother so uncertain. She

snatched on the familiar name. "You said Miles Clifton—"

"Yes, I know you learned about him in school," Ma said. "What's the story again?"

"He built the first cabin in Clifton in 1825, invited other people to live here, then moved on when he felt Clifton had become too civilized," Jessie said in the singsongy voice she used to answer Mr. Smythe. It was comforting to repeat the well-known history.

Ma laughed bitterly.

"That's so ridiculous. Miles Clifton couldn't survive two days in Clifton. He's a millionaire—he'd probably die without his limousine."

Jessie tried to understand.

"What's a millionaire? What's a limousine?"

"A millionaire is someone who's very rich. A limousine is a big car," Ma said. Jessie must have looked puzzled, because Ma went on. "And a car is—oh, Jessie, this is too hard! There's so much you need to know, and so much even I can't tell you—"

Ma looked like she was going to cry. Jessie felt frozen. She swallowed hard.

"Tell me what you do know," she said, trying to sound calm.

Ma nodded, and soon she went on, her tone as even as when she explained the multiplication tables to Nathan.

"Miles Clifton did found this village, in a way. He came up with the idea of building an authentic historical preserve, instead of doing it halfway, like at Williamsburg."

"Williamsburg? The old capital of Virginia?" Jessie asked, hoping she'd recognized another name. Maybe she wasn't as ignorant as Ma thought.

"Well, yes—you would know that, wouldn't you?"

"Mr. Smythe's from Virginia, remember, and he talks like it's really the only state in the Union."

"That's right. Only Williamsburg pretty much fell to pieces after the capital was moved. Then it was restored years ago as a tourist site." Again, Jessie felt confused, but this time Ma added the explanation smoothly. "A tourist site is someplace people travel to, to look at. Sometimes they go to learn something—Williamsburg was restored to help people understand the past. But mainly people go to tourist sites just for fun."

Jessie tried to make sense of that. Traveling was so difficult, she couldn't imagine people doing it to learn about the past. Didn't they have history books? And traveling just for fun would be crazy. All the adults in Clifton talked about how terrible their journeys out from the East had been. Except—Jessie herself had always wondered if the rest of the world looked like Clifton. It might be fun to find out.

Ma was still talking. It seemed that in Williamsburg and the other historical "tourist sites," people just pretended to live there, in that time period. Then they went home at the end of each day to twentieth-century lives. And tourists in shorts and tank tops—"strange twentieth-century clothing," Ma explained—had packed the streets of the tourist sites, killing all the historical feeling.

"So Miles Clifton wanted someplace where people lived twenty-four hours a day, year-round, and the tourists were hidden," Ma said.

Ma paused. Jessie wrapped and unwrapped one bonnet string around her finger. She was missing something in Ma's explanation. . . . Then she understood. She jerked back, hitting her head on the King of the Mountain rock.

"You mean—people watch us?"

Looking down, Ma nodded.

"All the time?"

"No, but—a lot. Oh, Jessie, I'm sorry. I'm trying to think how this must sound to you. It's terrible that you've been watched all these years and never knew it. And that's the part of Clifton we all agreed to, before things got worse—"

Jessie stopped listening. She was thinking about all the things she'd done that she wouldn't have wanted anyone else to see. Once when she was really little, she'd stolen a piece of barley candy from Mr. Seward's counter. But she felt so horrible, she took it back when no one was looking. And when Andrew was still too young to talk, she'd slapped him while Ma's back was turned, because Jessie hated everyone cooing over what a cute baby he was. And then there'd been other times, when she'd been alone or just with Mary, and they'd done dumb things like making faces at trees or doing imitations of all the adults in Clifton—Mr. Smythe as a bear, Mrs. Seward as a peacock. No one else was supposed to see those things. The people called tourists were watching her then, too?

For the first time in her life, Jessie wanted to scream at Ma. But Ma looked so worried and sad that Jessie couldn't. Jessie felt her anger ebb.

"Well, you always did tell us that God saw everything we did," Jessie said weakly.

Ma laughed.

"We tried to emphasize that. Would you have obeyed any

better if we'd said, 'God and lots of people you don't know'?"

Jessie shrugged, thinking hard.

"But how? How do these 'tourists' see us?"

"The mirrors in all the buildings work kind of like, oh, telescopes, I guess. That's not my area of science."

In a confusing way, Ma explained that the mirrors looked ordinary to everyone in Clifton, but they also carried images to people watching in rooms below the village. Some buildings had false backs, too, that people could watch through. And throughout the village, there were hidden things called video cameras and microphones.

"The tree," Jessie said suddenly, remembering. "That must have been a camera in the one haunted tree."

She recalled the glint of glass, and the spanking she'd received for trying to get a closer look.

"Yes. You shouldn't have been spanked for that, but—it was to protect you," Ma said.

"From what?"

Ma took Jessie's hand, cautioning her to wait for the rest of the story.

When Miles Clifton announced in the 1980s that he was looking for about twenty-five families willing to live like their great-great-grandparents, there was a lot of speculation about who would be interested, Ma said.

"People predicted a lot of crazies—and maybe they were right," Ma said. "Some people volunteered for Clifton because they thought the United States had become very sinful. They thought they could practice their religion better in the 1800s. Some people were running away from something in their twentieth-century lives. Others were environmentalists."

"En-vi-ron-mental-ists?" Jessie tried out the long word.

"People who were concerned about the way men were destroying the earth. Most of them ended up leaving. Some weren't willing to live so primitively. Others found America in the early 1800s was even more wasteful than in the 1980s."

"What about you and Pa?" Jessie asked.

"Pa, I think, was the only person who just plain wanted to live in the 1800s. And I—I was too much in love with him to tell him no," Ma finished in a husky voice.

Jessie looked away, out into the dark woods. Ma and Pa didn't talk about love much.

Pa had worked in a historical village in Massachusetts, learning how to be a blacksmith, Ma explained. He got really good at it, but there wasn't much call for blacksmithing in the 1980s.

Jessie couldn't understand that—blacksmiths did everything—but she let Ma go on.

Ma had been a nurse, which was kind of like a doctor, but there weren't any nurses in the early 1800s. So she gave that up.

"But you still take care of sick people," Jessie said.

"Not the way they should be taken care of. Medicine's much better in the future." She laughed bitterly. "Did I say 'future'? It's finally gotten to me!"

Jessie couldn't get used to Ma sounding like that. She reached out and touched Ma's face. It was wet. Jessie had never seen her mother cry.

Ma looked up, and Jessie could see her tears glistening in the lamplight. It scared her. She wondered if Ma had gone mad. What if this were all some story Ma had made up? It seemed like a lot to make up.

Ma saw Jessie looking at her, and pulled her into a hug.

"Oh, Jessie, I'm sorry. I don't like seeing you so terrified. Pa and I never knew what a nightmare this would turn into."

Although the tourists saw things as they were in the early 1800s, the people of Clifton at first had life much easier. Miles Clifton promised they would get modern medical care when they needed it. And in drought years, food was shipped in, so no one would starve. People were allowed to leave when they wanted to, and they were supposed to be able to tell their children the truth about Clifton when they turned twelve.

"We wanted you all to have a choice, to make your own decision about what century you wanted to live in."

"But—I'm thirteen," Jessie said. "You never told me . . . and I'm sure Hannah and Mary and Chester and Richard don't know either—"

"Things changed," Ma said. Again, her voice was bitter.

Gradually Miles Clifton took away everything that wasn't "authentic," as he called it. The modern medicine had stopped only six months earlier. But years before that, people were forbidden to leave or to mention the outside world as it really was. Adults weren't supposed to talk about the twentieth century with one another, let alone with their children. All the entrances to and exits from Clifton were sealed or guarded. The cameras—which were originally limited to only designated spots—appeared everywhere, to watch everything the Clifton residents did or said. And people were punished for anything that didn't fit Miles Clifton's idea of the early 1800s.

"*That's* what's wrong with 'okay' and 'shut up,' " Ma said. "People said those words all the time in the 1980s, and it was hard to break the habit. So you children picked it up, and you didn't understand—"

"I always asked about it," Jessie said, remembering what a pest she'd been. "And you got in trouble?"

"They beat Pa."

Jessie remembered a time Pa had come home with a black eye and bruises all over. He said he'd been kicked by a horse, but there was too much blood on his back.

"Oh, Ma—"

"It wasn't your fault. But that should let you know the danger you face."

FIVE

"**S**o I will have to do something dangerous," Jessie said. After hearing about Clifton's real past and the United States' future (for Jessie couldn't help thinking of it that way), she had almost forgotten the "something dangerous."

"Yes, I'm afraid so," Ma said grimly. "I think it's time to tell you about that."

"Wait, Ma, what about—"

Jessie wanted to ask so many questions, she couldn't think where to begin. She wanted to know about the "something dangerous," but she wanted to understand everything else Ma had told her first. She would have liked to take a day or two just to think. She wanted to go back to their cabin and look closely at the mirror on their back wall, to see how it was attached and how it divided her life and that other world of—what had Ma called them?—"tourists." She wanted to climb the haunted tree and finally examine the glass Ma said was a camera. She wanted to watch Pa and Mr. Smythe and the Ruddles and all the other adults in Clifton to see what they were hiding.

"Jessie, I know you're curious, but there's not much time," Ma said. "Can you just listen?"

Jessie nodded, dazed.

Ma pulled up the bag she always took on her midwife visits, and Jessie saw that it bulged more than usual.

"I wasn't supposed to save these, but I always thought there might come a time . . . I wish I hadn't been right," Ma said as she opened the bag.

Ma reached inside and pulled out a pair of trousers made of fabric Jessie had never seen before.

"Blue jeans," Ma said.

"Are these Pa's?"

"No, they were mine. In the 1980s, everyone wore blue jeans—men and women and children. . . . I just hope they're still 'in' in 1996."

Jessie and Ma both stared at the pants. They had pockets with shiny brass rivets that reflected the light from Ma's lamp. At the front, two rows of metal teeth peeked out from behind a cloth flap. Jessie reached out and felt the bottom where the pant leg flared out slightly. The material was softer than it looked, maybe because the blue jeans were made for a woman. Jessie had never heard of women wearing pants. But these trousers were so odd that Jessie began to believe the world outside Clifton was truly very different. She trembled, afraid. Before, she could half believe that Ma was making up the whole story. But these pants were proof, alien compared with everything Jessie was used to in Clifton.

"They look so strange, now!" Ma said, with a laugh that caught a little and sounded sad. "In the 1970s, everyone wore something called bell-bottoms, where the legs really opened out, but by the time we came into Clifton, legs were narrower again. Oh, I hadn't thought of bell-bottoms in years! It seems like another world. . . ."

She was crying again, but brushed away her tears.

"You'll need to wear the jeans and this T-shirt"—Ma pulled out a strange-looking shirt—"to go outside Clifton for help."

Somehow, in some part of Jessie's mind, she had known Ma was leading up to that. But Jessie still felt dizzy. She would have been a little scared of leaving Clifton even if she still thought it was 1840. But now . . . even Ma couldn't tell her what 1996 was like.

"Ma—" Jessie was ashamed that the word came out as a whimper.

"I know. If you're too scared—"

"I'm not!" Jessie said.

Ma smiled sadly. "I'm scared enough for both of us, then. Jessie—sending you out of Clifton is our last resort. We've tried everything else. We thought the quarantine signs would force Clifton's men to get us medicine before the tourists could see the signs. But they just ordered us to take the signs down, and threatened us."

"Clifton's men?"

"The ones who are on his side. Seward, the doctor, a few others."

Jessie considered that.

"Well, if they don't want these tourists finding out, and the tourists are watching us all the time anyway, why don't people just start talking about the sickness and needing medicine, and—"

Jessie was wound up, but Ma shook her head.

"We never know when the tourists are here and when they're not. We can't run the risk of being so bold, because— Jessie, I believe they might kill, rather than have their secrets out."

A chill crawled down Jessie's back.

"What if they catch me?" she asked in a small voice. It was hard dark in the woods now. Jessie stayed a little outside the lamp's glow so Ma wouldn't see how terrified she was.

Ma shook her head.

"Don't get caught." Ma looked down, then back at Jessie, her eyes burning. "I hate doing this to you. I've been turning this over in my mind all day, trying to think of another way. I wanted to go myself, but I can't fit in my old clothes anymore, not after having Andrew and Nathan and Bartholomew and Katie. I squeezed and squeezed trying to pull them on. So did Mrs. Ruddle and Mrs. Webster. We're all too fat—any of us who might go. And we'd be spotted in an instant in our Clifton clothes outside. So—that leaves you."

In spite of the danger, Jessie felt a rush of pride, that her mother trusted her instead of Hannah or anyone else.

"Won't everyone know I'm missing?" Jessie asked. "If I'm not at school tomorrow—"

"I thought of that. I'll just tell people you and Katie are both sick. I won't even tell Pa the truth. Pa"—Ma's voice cracked—"I love him very much, but I think he's forgotten this isn't 1840. At first I thought he was protecting me, not letting me speak of, of anything else. Now . . . it's different."

Jessie put her hand on Ma's shoulder and it struck her that that was something Ma would have done to comfort Jessie.

"Ma, that's all right. I can go. I'm good at being brave. Remember?" Jessie's voice sounded scared to her, but Ma smiled.

"Yes. I can count on you."

Ma gave her a package of things to carry and told her what she had planned. Ma thought a man named Isaac Neeley could help. He had opposed the founding of Clifton, saying it was unethical. He lived in Indianapolis.

"I have to walk to Indianapolis?" Jessie asked. She knew Indiana's capital was about thirty or forty miles away.

"No," Ma said. "If we're lucky, you won't have to walk very far at all. You need to get out of Clifton and find a pay phone to call Mr. Neeley. I've written his number on a piece of paper in this package."

Ma explained a little more—what a phone looked like, how a phone worked, where to put the money. Jessie listened, but it seemed too incredible. How could she stand by a box just outside Clifton and talk to someone in Indianapolis, forty miles away? It was crazy.

"Do you understand?" Ma asked.

Jessie nodded. But she thought that if she had to talk to this Mr. Neeley, she'd have to walk to Indianapolis first.

"What do I tell him?" Jessie asked.

"Tell him there's a diphtheria epidemic in Clifton and the authorities are refusing to treat the patients with anything but 1840s medicine," Ma said. "Tell him—tell him children are going to die if they don't get help."

The words stunned Jessie.

"Katie? Betsy?" She almost wailed.

"I don't know. I hope I'm wrong and they all get well. But Jefferson Webster and Abby Harlow are very, very ill, and some of the others may be as bad soon. I'm only telling you this so you know how serious it is—many people died of diphtheria before there was medicine to treat it. And this appears to be a particularly virulent strain. You were all supposed to be vaccinated against diphtheria, but Dr. Fister must have lied to us about that."

"But why?" Jessie asked. "Why would anyone want children to die?"

Ma shook her head.

"That's one of the things I don't understand either. At first, everything was done to be authentic—but this is too much. I wondered if the world outside Clifton had changed, and there isn't medicine available anymore. But I'm almost certain Susan Seward is getting treatment."

"Because Mr. Seward is on Miles Clifton's side?"

Ma nodded grimly.

"Jessie, I'm sending you into a puzzle. It's been twelve years since I've been outside Clifton myself, and Mr. Clifton's men act so strangely. . . . I've tried to figure everything out, but I can't. Maybe Mr. Neeley will be able to explain. I just know we can't let Abby or Jefferson or—or Katie—or anyone die when there is medicine out there."

The lamp flickered, and Jessie heard an owl far away. She tried to think of the words to reassure Ma, but they wouldn't come. All Jessie could think of was more questions.

"How will Mr. Neeley get the medicine to Clifton?" Jessie asked. "If Mr. Clifton and his men won't let him in—"

"Oh, he won't bring it himself. He'll call the board of health and cause a big fuss." Ma sounded more confident, as though she was sure she could trust Mr. Neeley. She even chuckled a little. "And, if I had him figured right, he'll probably call a news conference, too."

Jessie wanted to ask what a news conference was, but she had begun to feel impatient to begin her journey. It was like the time she'd walked the log across Crooked Creek—she knew if she waited too long she might chicken out. So she asked a more important question.

"How do I get out of Clifton?"

Ma smiled.

"When you children began playing on this rock, Miles Clifton's men got so upset that a couple of us decided we'd better look at it. At first we thought they were mad because it seemed to be the only place in Clifton out of range of the cameras and microphones. Then we discovered—it's a way out that isn't sealed."

Ma showed Jessie a thin crack under the rock.

"But—there are guards?" Jessie asked.

"Yes. You have to be careful and avoid them."

"But—"

"I know," Ma said. Her voice was sympathetic, then turned brusque, the way it did when Nathan or Bartholomew asked for more food, and there wasn't any. "Get changed and I'll help you through."

Jessie looked at the strange clothes Ma called blue jeans

and a T-shirt, and swallowed a lump in her throat. She took off her bonnet and handed it to Ma, then began unbuttoning her dress. The night air was cold on her skin and she slipped quickly into the shirt. It had short sleeves and wasn't much protection.

"Here. I have a windbreaker, too," Ma said.

Jessie put on the strange coat, which was slippery and had long rows of teethlike bumps along the front edges.

"It's made of something called nylon, and that's a zipper in front," Ma said, showing Jessie how to fasten it.

Jessie thought she must look odd, with her woolen dress still hooked around her waist and the nylon jacket at the top. She sat down and took off her boots, then pulled off her dress and petticoat. Ma slipped the dress over a long branch.

"I'm going to carry this to the cabin so people will think I'm bringing you back from the woods," she explained.

"That's smart," Jessie said as she pulled on the blue jeans. The pants' metal teeth, it turned out, were also a zipper. The trousers were a little too big, but felt stiff around Jessie's legs. Ma handed Jessie a pair of shoes she called sneakers—funny things made of cloth, with a sole that bent. But they flapped on Jessie's feet no matter how tightly Ma tried to tie them.

"You'll have to keep your boots, because you may have to walk a mile or so to find a phone. I hope nobody notices your feet."

Jessie put her square-toed boots back on and stood up. She felt different, freer. But she missed the loose skirt around her legs.

Ma pulled her back down to whisper, "You should unbraid your hair. I don't know what the styles are now. You might have to cut it to fit in when you see. We don't want anyone guessing you're from Clifton."

Jessie yanked the pins out of her hair and it came down wavy from the braids. Ma held the lamp up to look at Jessie.

"Well, you don't look like 1840 anymore. You don't look like 1984 either. Let's hope you'll do okay in 1996."

Ma put down the lamp and hugged Jessie long and hard. Jessie felt like crying, but she squeezed back the tears. She'd told Ma she was brave. Now she had to be.

"Be careful, little one," Ma said. Then she turned and began digging at the crack at the bottom of the rock. In a little bit, Jessie saw a round piece of rough metal. She could make out the letters MANHOLE across the rim. Ma pulled a handle at one side. Moving the lamp, Jessie could see a rusty iron ladder leading into darkness below.

Ma kissed Jessie's forehead and handed her the package to carry.

"Go on, and I'll cover the hole," Ma said.

Jessie started down the steps. The rungs of the ladder were mossy and slick. Jessie hesitated halfway down.

"Shouldn't I take a lamp?" she asked. Ma held her own lamp near the hole, but its light was weak and didn't reach the bottom of the steps.

"No," Ma said. "That would give you away."

Jessie didn't understand, but she kept climbing into the dark. Finally she felt the ground under her feet and began edging cautiously into the blackness.

"Have you found the door?" Ma asked softly from above.

The tip of Jessie's boot scraped something and Jessie reached out her hand. She felt smooth metal and then a knob, also smooth. What kind of blacksmith made things that even and unblemished? Jessie's pa was good—everyone said so—but even his best work had some bumps and pockmarks.

"I think this is it," Jessie whispered.

"Good. I've got to leave now." Jessie could hear the tears in her mother's voice. "Godspeed."

Jessie didn't trust her voice enough to reply. In seconds Ma had re-covered the hole, and everything was black.

Jessie turned the knob.

SIX

Remembering Ma's warning about guards, Jessie pushed the door open slowly. When the crack between the door and the wall was wide enough, she peeked out.

The door led to a long, dimly lit corridor. No one was in sight, so Jessie stepped out and shut the door.

The floor of the corridor was smooth and shiny, with a pattern of alternating black and white squares. They glistened, even in the dim light. To think: This had been down here the whole time Jessie lived in Clifton! Jessie had never seen a floor that wasn't wood or dirt, so she bent down and felt it. She loved it—until she began walking. Her boots clattered so loudly she had to tiptoe.

The lights in the corridor didn't flicker at all—not like any candle or lamp Jessie had ever seen. She wasn't tall enough to reach the globes that lit the hall every fifty feet or so, or she would have felt them, too. As far as she could tell, the globes held no flame. How could there be light without fire? Jessie wanted to go back and ask Ma, but resisted. Somehow she knew she'd have lots of questions, the longer she was away from home. Maybe Mr. Neeley could answer some of them. The rest she'd save for when she got back to Clifton.

In spite of the sickness in Clifton and the mystery and danger Ma said she faced, Jessie felt a rising excitement. She was only a few minutes into her journey, and had already seen a miracle: flameless light. What more might she see? How could Ma and Pa have left such an amazing world?

And then Jessie saw two men way down the hall. Pressing against the wall, Jessie wished the light was a little less steady.

"—going to patrol there?" one man was asking.

The other man glanced down the hall, and Jessie felt he was looking right at her.

"Okay. You do the other end," he said. "Did you punch in?"

"Oh, thanks. I forgot. Knowing them, they wouldn't pay me if I was five minutes late."

Both men passed out of sight. A minute later, Jessie heard a click down the long hall. What were they punching?

The men's voices were too low to hear now. Had they seen her, or heard her footsteps before she stopped? Jessie didn't think so, but her heart pounded so loudly she couldn't believe they couldn't hear *that*. For a minute, she stood frozen, too scared to move. These had to be the guards Ma had warned her about. They mustn't find her. She had to hide before they patrolled this hall.

Tiptoeing as quickly and quietly as she could, Jessie raced

back to the door she'd come through only a few moments before. She turned the knob every way she could, but the door didn't give. Frantically, she tried jerking it, yanking it, pushing it.

It was locked. It must have locked behind her.

Jessie peered up and down the corridor. Its smooth walls seemed unbroken—but wait, straight down from this door there was a gaping darkness. Jessie wasn't sure what it was. Her only hope, she thought.

Jessie rushed toward the darkness. Behind her, she heard one of the men whistling off-key. She might have laughed at him if Ma's words weren't echoing in her head: "I believe they might kill, rather than have their secrets out." She was sure the man was walking down the corridor now, though she was too scared to turn around and look. His steps were loud and fast; any minute now he'd be close enough to see her.

Inches from the dark opening, Jessie took a chance and leaped.

"Hey! Who's there?" the guard yelled. His footsteps stopped, as though he was listening.

In the safe darkness, Jessie let out a silent breath. The guard would have to go back for a lantern now, she thought, and she'd have time to figure out what to do.

"Hey, Ernie," the man called out. "Hit the lights, will you?"

Almost instantly, the corridor was flooded with bright light. It seemed the man had turned on some kind of inside sun. Jessie suddenly wasn't so fond of the miracle globes of flameless light. She had to think fast. She was still in a dark area, but enough light shone in from the corridor that she could see the tinker's cart, a stagecoach, and a buggy like the one visiting politicians used. There were also hoes, rakes, and a wheelbarrow. Absently, Jessie realized that the tinker, the stagecoach driver, and the politicians must only pretend to live in the 1800s when they visited Clifton: This was where their Clifton things were stored. But that didn't matter now—where could she hide? Jessie saw a pile of burlap bags by the door. Was that the best place? Or was it the place the guards would look first?

Jessie remembered a time she and Andrew had hidden under the stagecoach for a prank, planning to ride out a few miles before they jumped out and scared the passengers. They'd been found then, but the stagecoach looked like the best place to hide now.

Moving quickly, Jessie dived under the stagecoach and crawled up by the wheel axles. She tucked her hair into the collar of her coat, afraid it would hang down and give her away. Clinging to the axle, she realized she'd left her package on the ground. She reached down for it just as the bright light burst into the room.

"Well, I'll be—Ernie, someone left the storage room open," the guard said.

"Maintenance always forgets," the other one said. "I had to lock it last night, too. But—what'd you hear?"

"Who knows? Mice? Look around."

Jessie heard the men pacing the large room. One kicked the pile of bags by the door, and Jessie was glad she hadn't hidden there. The other guard opened the doors of the stage-coach and buggy. By the stagecoach, his foot was close enough Jessie could have reached down and touched it. She held her breath. Her arms ached from clutching the axle, but she just tightened her grip. She couldn't be found. She couldn't. Why wouldn't the men leave?

They pounded the wheelbarrow, kicked over the hoes and rakes. Jessie was sure her arms were going to give out. They began to tremble dangerously. Jessie felt dizzy from the lack of air, but was too scared to breathe.

"Must have been mice," the first guard finally said.

"They should put out traps. Or poison."

"Yeah. Ready for coffee?"

The light went out again, and the door slammed. Jessie heard the guards' footsteps echo down the corridor. She gulped in fresh air, but for a long time was afraid to let go of the axle. With the door shut and the lights out, the room was totally dark. But Jessie kept seeing awful visions of herself being caught. She almost had been. What would have happened to her? What would have happened to Katie and all the other children who needed her to get help?

Finally Jessie's arms went numb and she dropped to the ground. She still crouched under the stagecoach, in case the men came back. Her ears roared from listening so hard to the silence. Was it safe to leave? Ma had said she should hide during the night in something called a rest room, which Ma described as an indoor outhouse. In the morning, when the tourists came in, Jessie could just walk out of the rest room like one of them. Jessie had thought how much easier the chore of emptying the chamber pots would be if she didn't have to go outdoors. But she had wondered how people could stand the smell of an outhouse inside.

Now, all she could think about was how she'd have to walk

the whole length of the corridor to get to the rest room. What if she just stayed under the stagecoach? But no—it would look suspicious if she was found in this room in the morning. And Ma knew a lot more about the outside world than Jessie did. This wasn't a good time to disobey.

Reluctantly, Jessie crawled from under the stagecoach and inched toward the door. She listened at the door, heard nothing, then turned the knob. The door shut behind her and she knew it was locked, just like the first door. She had to get down the corridor without being seen or heard this time. Otherwise—Jessie didn't let herself finish the thought.

It seemed an eternity before Jessie reached a huge room at the end of the hall. Her ankles ached from the effort of tiptoeing. The whole hall slanted up ever so slightly; Jessie thought she might be at ground level by the end. Ma had explained that was how the tourist part of Clifton was designed—though she'd never been there, she remembered the diagrams when Clifton was first built. Ma said the big room was where tourists gathered during the day. Jessie peeked around the corner, hoping no one was in the room at night. But the guards were. They were sitting at a table at the far side of the enormous room. Coffee, Jessie remembered. They were drinking coffee.

Jessie ducked back around the corner. Panic welled up in her. There was nowhere to hide now. All they had to do was walk this way and they'd see her.

"—heard they're hiring over at Ryan Industries," one guard was saying.

"Yeah? How much?"

"Nine dollars an hour."

The other man whistled.

"What shift?"

"Second."

"You applied?"

"Wilma wants me to. I'm going to look into it. Especially now they're getting so picky here. . . . You'd think we were guarding a prison."

"Wouldn't you want out, if you was those people? 'Sides, they never said we was supposed to look for escapees."

"What else we looking for? Ever heard of so many guards at a place like this?"

"I don't know. . . . Did I tell you? Jack said they're going to close this place soon, anyhow. No more tourists, no more freaky people living in the past, no more paychecks for us."

"That rumor's been going around for years. . . ."

Jessie didn't hear the other man's answer. What did he mean, close the place? Why wouldn't there be any more tourists? What would happen to everyone in Clifton? It was a puzzle Jessie didn't have time to worry about. She stored the idea with all the mysterious things Ma had told her, to think about later. She risked another look around the corner. And then she saw it, not far along the wall in the opposite direction from the two men: a sign that said REST ROOMS, with an arrow.

Jessie *thought* it was dark enough on that side of the room that they wouldn't see her. And there were enough tables between her and them. . . . She decided to crawl.

Strapping her package around her neck, Jessie crouched along the wall. Each motion took great nerve. She wished she'd stayed by the stagecoach. She wished Ma had picked someone else to leave Clifton. Andrew, maybe. She wished Katie and the others had never gotten sick. She wished she'd never heard of the world outside Clifton. She wished Ma and Pa had never moved to Clifton, but stuck with whatever happened in the twentieth century.

Wishing all that, Jessie reached the sign with the arrow and followed the arrow down a short hall. There were two doors. Looking up, Jessie could see the word LADIES on one, with a small silhouette of a woman in a bonnet and long dress, like Ma or any of the other women in Clifton might wear. The sight comforted Jessie. The silhouette was etched in a strange hard substance, but Jessie didn't take the time to marvel at it.

She pushed open the door and went to sit on an odd white chair that matched her mother's description of a "toilet." It would not be a comfortable place to sleep, but Ma had insisted.

Jessie crossed her legs up on the toilet, as Ma had directed, and leaned her head against the smooth metal wall around the toilet. She had made it safely. The guards hadn't caught her. Her terror slipped away, and she fell asleep wondering how this indoor outhouse could be used more than once, since the toilet was so shallow.

SEVEN

W*hoosh!*
Jessie woke to an awful sound of rushing water. She remembered learning about the Niagara Falls in geography—was this what they sounded like?

Confused by the noise, at first Jessie couldn't remember where she was and why she wasn't sleeping cozily in the bed she shared with Hannah. Her whole body ached from trying to balance on the white porcelain chair—the toilet—all night. She wondered if it was safe to move yet. The room was as bright as midday, but Jessie couldn't see any windows. So it was those globe things again, putting out more light than Jessie had ever seen from a candle or a lamp. Even though the lights had almost led to her capture the night before, now that she was safe, she decided once again that they were incredible.

"Heather, is that the ring Jason gave you?"

"Yeah. Like it?"

The voices came from in front of Jessie's little metal stall. She was so eager to see what real 1996 girls looked like that she knocked her elbow against the back of her toilet getting up.

Whoosh!

This time the sound came from her toilet. The water swirled powerfully, then disappeared. In a few moments, more came pouring in from the back. Jessie watched it in amazement and felt the pipes that led to the wall. So that was why the toilet hole wasn't very deep. But where did the water go?

Jessie decided it was too much of a mystery. She went to the door she'd fastened so carefully the night before. Through a crack, she could see three girls standing before a mirror. One had her hand held out for the other two to see. All three girls had hair as wild as Jessie's, and Jessie grinned. Her hair fit in without her having to do a thing with it! For the first time she could remember, she could get up in the morning without trying to braid her hair.

Jessie tried to see what the girls were wearing, to compare with her own clothes. But it was hard to tell through the narrow crack. And while Jessie was peering out, the girls finished admiring Heather's ring and left.

Jessie wanted to follow them, but first she wanted to find an outhouse. She started to unfasten her door, then remembered she didn't have to. Minutes later, she pushed the *whoosh* lever and felt quite proud that she'd figured out 1996.

Finally stepping out of her stall, Jessie faced the mirror. It was enormous, stretching the entire length of the wall. And unlike all the mirrors in Clifton, it was clear and undistorted.

For the first time in her life, Jessie saw herself without waves and lines and blotches.

Half fearing this might be another mirror people watched through, Jessie still stared in fascination. Her dark hair, unbraided, swirled around her head like a cloud. Digging through the bag Ma had given her, Jessie pulled out a wooden comb and began yanking it through her tangles. She went slowly, preoccupied with gazing in the mirror. Her eyes, she saw for the first time, were exactly the same color as Pa's in sunlight: greenish with flecks of hazel. But hers were impatient, curious, and she had never seen his look that way.

Standing back far enough to see her jacket and jeans, Jessie examined herself carefully so she would be able to compare herself with the real 1996 people. The coat Ma called a windbreaker was kind of pretty, even though it looked boyish. She unzipped it far enough to see the thing Ma called a T-shirt. It was yellow and had a huge black circle imprinted on it, with a line and two dots inside. It sort of looked like a smiling face, maybe on some stick figure Katie or one of the other little children drew in the dust.

While Jessie was staring at herself, she heard another *whoosh* and a girl stepped out from one of the other bathroom stalls. Jessie pretended to concentrate on combing her hair, but watched the girl carefully. She had fluffy blond hair that stood straight out from the sides of her face, almost as though it had been frozen in the wind. Her pants were the things Ma called blue jeans, but they were faded and much tighter than Jessie's. And her purple flowered top looked nothing like Jessie's T-shirt. Patting her hair, the girl stepped to a counter in front of the mirror and turned a knob. Water gushed out of a shiny metal loop.

"What's wrong? Never seen anybody wash their hands before?" the girl asked.

Jessie didn't know what to say. Could the girl tell Jessie wasn't used to the twentieth century? Would she summon the guards?

Before Jessie could come up with a good answer, the girl shrugged, pulled a sheet of paper out of a nearby container, wiped off her hands, and threw the paper into a can. Then she left, as though she didn't care why Jessie had been staring.

Jessie didn't think the girl was going to tell anyone about her. Still, she decided she'd better leave the bathroom. But first, she tried turning the same knob, and again water came pouring out. What a place this world-outside-Clifton was!

After following the same ritual as the girl before her—even throwing away the paper, as crazy as that seemed—Jessie stepped out into the giant room she'd been in the night before.

The largest room Jessie had ever seen before this one was Seward's store, and it was always crowded with spices, cloth, barrels, and everything else Clifton needed. Only five or six people could fit inside comfortably at one time. This room was open and airy, with glass in the ceiling that let in bright sunlight. About the only furniture was a cluster of tables and chairs at the other end, where the guards had had coffee the night before. But the room was hardly empty: It was packed with people. Maybe two hundred, Jessie calculated in amazement, more than in all of Clifton. And many of them appeared to be about Jessie's age. They sat along the walls, milled around in the open areas, hovered over the tables.

Anxious to fit in, Jessie couldn't help staring as she'd stared at the girl in the bathroom. Many of the other children wore blue jeans, but some jeans were a darker blue than Jessie's, and some were faded almost white. Some were skintight and some were so loose it seemed miraculous that they didn't fall off.

Jessie thought maybe her jeans looked okay.

The other children's shirts and jackets were very different, though, many with bright patterns that almost glowed. Jessie's top definitely stood out. But no one else seemed to notice. No one looked at Jessie at all. The other children were too busy talking, laughing, and even screaming.

"—and then he goes—"

"Who you going out with tonight?"

"—and we were at the mall and then—"

Jessie had never heard so many voices at once. It hurt her ears. It would be easy to leave unnoticed, she decided, but she leaned against the wall for a minute longer, trying to get used to all the noise.

"Kids, come on. It's your turn for the tour."

Jessie turned and saw a woman about her mother's age, dressed in brown pants like a man. She was talking to the group around Jessie. Jessie noticed that the girl called Heather was right beside her.

Most of the others got up, but Heather and her friends still sat. Jessie decided to wait a minute before leaving.

"Oh no, you guys, too," the woman said. Heather and the other two stood up, complaining. The woman looked at Jessie.

"Why aren't you coming? Do you expect me to carry you?"

"But—" Jessie started. The woman thought she was with the other girls! It was on the tip of Jessie's tongue to explain that she wasn't, but the woman was glaring like Mr. Smythe always did before he said, "Do you want a whipping?" Jessie looked around. She didn't see any guards, but they might be just around the corner. What if the woman yelled for one? What if the woman started asking just where Jessie did belong? What if "Clifton's men" found out where she was?

Jessie tried to look innocent.

"I'm coming, ma'am," she said.

The woman gave Jessie a surprised look, but Jessie followed along, looking meekly at the ground.

It appeared she was going to be one of those things called tourists.

EIGHT

The woman who had herded Jessie and the others together walked right behind Jessie, so there was no chance to break off and escape.

"Teenagers!" the woman snorted. The word sounded vaguely familiar to Jessie. She thought it might be like "okay" and "shut up," another word from the future not allowed in Clifton. But why did the woman say it so angrily?

Jessie gave up wondering and looked around. They were heading down the same corridor Jessie had crept through the night before. But in the bright light from those miraculous glass globes, now Jessie noticed pictures on the wall. Moving slowly toward them, Jessie saw they weren't paintings or drawings but something else, something that seemed to capture scenes just as someone might see them. They were incredible. How could such pictures exist?

Jessie remembered Mr. Smythe telling the school about a new invention called a daguerreotype, but she'd only half believed him. It sounded crazy, that someone's image could be captured like that. And, of course, she'd never actually seen a daguerreotype. The first one in the United States had been taken only the year before, in 1839. Maybe that's what these were. Why, she'd be the first person in Clifton to—

Suddenly Jessie realized how silly she was being. Everyone else walked by the pictures as though they were nothing. The rest of the world had seen hundreds of these daguerreotypes, probably. She had to remember this was 1996, not 1840.

Then Jessie noticed all these scenes were from Clifton: Mrs. Harlow cooking over the open fireplace, Mr. Seward measuring out a poke of flour for Mrs. Ruddle, Mr. Smythe looking stern as the schoolchildren stood and recited. And yes—Jessie was in that picture, in the fifth-grade row. She looked younger, but it was definitely her.

Jessie looked around, wanting to tell someone how strange it was to see herself as she'd looked two years ago. But she couldn't. That was the last thing she should tell anyone.

Remembering the danger, Jessie moved away from the pictures. She tried to walk in the center of the group. Cautiously, so no one would catch her staring, she looked around at the others. And she got another jolt: A few of the children, she discovered, were actually Negroes! At least, their faces and hands were a shade or two darker than Jessie's. Some of them had curly hair, but others' hair was straight. Jessie had never seen a Negro, and she was disappointed that their skin wasn't pure black and their hair pure curl, as she'd always heard. Jessie didn't think they could be slaves, because they acted just like all the other children. Maybe the abolitionists in Clifton had gotten their wish, and there wasn't slavery anymore.

By this time, the group was beyond the door Jessie had come through the night before. A bit farther down the hall, Jessie saw a woman wearing a long dress, apron, and bonnet. It made Jessie feel better to see someone dressed like that, but the woman wasn't from Clifton.

The group of children reached the woman and she motioned for them to stop.

"Good morning!" she said, a little too cheerfully. "Welcome to Clifton. My name's Mrs. Spurning and I'm going to be your tour guide today. I understand you've come on a school trip from"—she looked at a card in her hand— "Oakdale Junior High School?"

Some of the children mumbled yeses. Any adult in Clifton would have reprimanded the children and ordered them to say, "Yes, ma'am," promptly and crisply. But this Mrs. Spurning only smiled.

"Well, we have quite a treat for you today. This will be like going back in a time machine. When you left for school this morning, it was 1996. Here, it's 1840. The people here live without TVs, VCRs, stereos, refrigerators, freezers, or even running water—"

"How do they survive?" one boy with spiky yellow hair asked. Several around him laughed.

Mrs. Spurning ignored his smart-alecky tone.

"They survive just like many of your ancestors did. Some would say they live better than you, because they aren't weighed down with your possessions."

"I doubt it," the boy said. The others laughed again.

Mrs. Spurning forced a smile. "Why don't you wait and see?"

She continued, speaking dully, as though she'd said the same words many times before. She sounded like Mr. Smythe when he repeated poetry at school. But Mrs. Spurning was describing the history of Clifton as Ma had the night before. Mrs. Spurning kept calling it "Clifton Village."

"Do the people here really think it's 1840?" a Negro girl with spectacles asked. She looked really smart. So Mr. Wittingham was wrong when he said Negroes couldn't think like white people.

Jessie listened carefully to Mrs. Spurning's answer.

"Oh, these people aren't crazy," Mrs. Spurning said with a laugh. "Only the youngest children think it's 1840. All the others are let in on Clifton Village's little secret as soon as they are old enough to understand. No one speaks of it, though, because they are happy here. And they do get some benefits of the twentieth century—medical care, for example. It would be inhumane to let anyone die of the diseases that many died of back then, when antibiotics are available now."

"But that's not—" Jessie started to protest. Everyone turned to look at her, and Jessie realized she couldn't call this woman a liar. Not now. No one would believe her.

"That's not, uh, authentic," Jessie finished lamely. She cleared her throat. "I'm not saying I want anyone to die, but how do we know this is really what 1840 was like?"

"Now, that's a good question, isn't it, children?" Mrs. Spurning said in a sticky-sweet tone. She seemed to be making fun of Jessie. "We could never be 100 percent sure, and things like twentieth-century medical care will always make Clifton Village a little different from any real village of 1840. But we've researched everything about this period, and Clifton Village is as authentic as possible. Now, do we want to talk about it or see it?"

She turned, obviously meaning for the children to follow her the rest of the way down the hall. As they trooped behind her, the girl with the spectacles came toward Jessie.

"She was sure mean to you," the girl said. "And it was a good question. I've been reading a lot about this period—people lived in really filthy conditions then, but I doubt if we see filth today."

"Oh," Jessie said. She would have liked to tell the girl everything, and ask her all about 1996. And ask her if slavery really had been abolished. But after almost giving herself away, she knew she had to be careful. The guards weren't chasing her anymore, but there was still danger. She wasn't allowed to relax until she told Mr. Neeley about the diphtheria and got medicine for Katie and the others.

"My name's Nicole," the girl was saying. "Nicole Stevens. My parents didn't have any imagination—there are two other Nicoles in my class."

"Oh," Jessie said again. She had never met anyone named Nicole. It was pretty. "I'm Jessie."

Mrs. Spurning saved Jessie from having to say anything else. She stopped the group and began explaining the system of mirrors and cameras that allowed them to see everything happening above ground. They were under the village square right now—she pointed to an image on a wide stretch of glass, and Jessie saw Mr. Harlow pull up his wagon to the store. It was like the pictures back on the walls of the corridor, only Mr. Harlow was moving like in real life. One of his horses was missing a shoe, and Jessie had to stop herself from yelling out to him to get it fixed. He walked into the store, seeming unaware that thirty children were watching him.

"Off to the side, through each of these doors, you can see what's happening in the various shops and in each of the houses. Our monitors tell us"—Mrs. Spurning glanced at a box above the group's heads—"there's bread being baked at Dr. Fister's house, the potter is making bowls, and the blacksmith—oh, you should see this. Come along."

She led the children to a door marked JOSEPH KEYSER, ESQ., BLACKSMITH.

Inside was a room with about fifty chairs, more than could fit in Pa's shop. But against one wall, full-length, was a clear image of Pa bent over a horseshoe glowing red. Jessie could hear the crackle of the fire behind him and see the sweat flowing down his face. For a minute, Jessie forgot she wasn't standing in the shop herself, perhaps having stopped in after school to see Pa. But she couldn't feel the heat of the fire, and all these strangely dressed future children surrounded her.

Some were snickering.

"Couldn't he find an easier way to do that?" one boy asked.

"Shut up!" Jessie said. "He's the best!"

NINE

"**W**ell," Mrs. Spurning said as everyone stared at Jessie. "I see the blacksmith has a fan."

Jessie bent her head, afraid she would say more and betray who she was. She wondered what the wood-vented fan in the corner of Pa's blacksmith shop had to do with what she had said. She concentrated on listening to Mrs. Spurning. And don't say *anything!* she warned herself.

"It's true," Mrs. Spurning continued, "that by 1840 standards, our blacksmith here is quite talented. It's just that you're used to seeing the products of much more advanced techniques."

Jessie heard mumblings around the boy who'd made fun of Pa, something like, "touchy, touchy." But she didn't look at him. The vision of Pa, now staring at another horseshoe, swam in front of Jessie's eyes.

"Don't mind them," Nicole leaned over to say. "They're stupid. If it's not on MTV, they don't know what it is."

Jessie nodded without understanding. She wished everyone would leave so she could step into Pa's shop and have everything be normal again. She wouldn't even mind being scolded for skipping school. But she had to think about Katie. . . .

"Hey, why are you with our group? I've never seen you at Oakdale," Nicole said.

"Oh, I don't go there. I, uh, got separated from my classmates," Jessie said, not really lying.

"Hope you don't get in trouble when you get back."

"Me too." Absolutely, Jessie thought.

Nicole was still looking at Jessie a little strangely, and Jessie was afraid she might guess Jessie really didn't belong. She crowded forward, pretending to be very intent on Mrs. Spurning's explanation of how vital a blacksmith was to an 1840s community. Mrs. Spurning couldn't say enough about how important Pa was, Jessie thought. She clenched her teeth to keep from adding things.

But in a few minutes, Mrs. Spurning had finished with Pa, and she led the group to the next room. There, the image was of Mr. Wittingham making barrels. He got a couple minutes of explanation, the children stared, and then it was on to the next room.

To Jessie, everything they saw looked achingly familiar. Many of the women were standing outside in their yards boiling their laundry, while others tended cooking pots over their fireplaces. The maid at Dr. Fister's polished his silver tea service. Mr. Seward measured out flour, sugar, and salt for Mrs. Green on his dented scales.

But the children around Jessie poked fun at almost everything.

"Hasn't she ever heard of a washing machine?" the girl called Heather said as they watched Mrs. Morrow expertly wring out a pair of long underwear.

"Look at that hat! Ug-ly!" another girl said about Mrs. Green's stylish bonnet. "She looks like a duck."

Jessie and her friends had made fun of Mrs. Green themselves—and she did look like a duck. But Jessie gritted her teeth to keep from saying something mean back. Didn't these girls know how silly they looked, wearing pants like boys?

Mrs. Spurning told Heather, no, in 1840 there was no such thing as a washing machine, and she should be glad they existed now. Jessie wondered what a washing machine was. Was it easier? She hated laundry.

When they had seen most of the rooms for the houses and shops, Mrs. Spurning brought the group back to the open area in the middle. Jessie saw several other groups behind them, working their way through the rooms Jessie's group had seen. All of them had guides like Mrs. Spurning, wearing what Jessie thought of as the right clothes. How many people watched Clifton every day?

"All right, kids, we're almost done," Mrs. Spurning said. "Before we see our last place, I want to remind you Clifton Village is open on weekends, so you can bring your parents back with you sometime when you want to stay longer. We also have special events, like the Fourth of July celebration and Christmas at Clifton. The next event is the revival on May 25, 26, and 27. I'm sure you'd enjoy that."

Jessie stared. Even the annual revivals—when Reverend Holloway rode in and preached for three hours a night, so vividly that Jessie always dreamed afterward of hellfire and brimstone—even those had an audience. Was there anything the tourists weren't allowed to see?

"You can pick up a schedule of special events at the ticket window," Mrs. Spurning continued. "And if you want to spend a day just watching Clifton, you can rent out spots on the town square." She pointed to a covered opening in the ceiling. "We put stairs there."

"Don't the Clifton people see you?" a boy asked.

"No. You're inside one of the three hollow trees we have up there. It's quite an experience."

Mrs. Spurning went on, but Jessie's mind blanked. Hollow trees . . . She meant the haunted trees! So they were haunted, in a way. Jessie shivered. She would have preferred ghosts.

". . . You have to reserve the lookouts way in advance, because anthropologists are beginning to flock to Clifton for those spots. It's a wonderful perspective on a primitive culture," Mrs. Spurning said.

Jessie glowered. Primitive culture! She'd like to see Mrs. Spurning work like Ma or any other woman in Clifton. As far as she could see, all Mrs. Spurning could do was talk. Jessie wanted to yell at Mrs. Spurning, as she had at the boy in the blacksmith shop. Think of Katie, she told herself. You can't because you have to get help for Katie. And Betsy. And Abby. And Jefferson. And . . .

Repeating the names calmed her, but she almost missed hearing a voice from behind her.

"Isn't this whole concept a little, well, a little voyeuristic?" Nicole asked.

Jessie didn't know what voyeuristic meant, and, from their puzzled expressions, it seemed a lot of the other children didn't either.

"Aren't we invading these people's privacy?" Nicole continued. "I mean, if they want to live like it's 1840, that's fine, but why should they let us watch them?"

Mrs. Spurning gave Nicole the same "Oh, aren't you precious" look she'd given Jessie when Jessie said the village wasn't authentic.

"When they moved here," Mrs. Spurning said slowly, "they agreed that they would be watched. In exchange, they are not bothered in their lifestyle. They have total privacy except in the common areas we've seen, and they know that. And, of course, they're free to leave whenever they want."

Nicole shrugged, giving up. But Jessie bit her tongue so hard she could taste blood, holding back from telling Nicole and Mrs. Spurning and everybody else the truth.

"Any more questions? No? Good. Because now we're going to see the school," Mrs. Spurning said.

Jessie hung back as the others surged through the door Mrs. Spurning held open. She didn't want to see these children make fun of her friends. But finally she had to step through because the other woman was staring at her again. The woman had told Mrs. Spurning she was a chaperon, not the teacher. Did she have a bigger name because she was meaner?

The chaperon glared as Jessie looked around. Jessie turned her gaze to Mrs. Spurning.

"This school focuses entirely on memorization and rote recitation," Mrs. Spurning said. "Pupils study and then repeat back what they have learned. That was considered the best way to educate a child in the early 1800s."

Jessie wondered how else someone could learn something, besides memorizing it.

"Listen now," Mrs. Spurning said. "I believe it's time for the first graders to recite."

The little children at the front stood. "Cat," they said, "c-a-t. Dog, d-o-g."

"Ant, a-n-t," Jessie muttered, so softly she was sure no one would hear. Katie had recited those words for Jessie just a few days ago, while Ma was busy listening to Bartholomew's geography recitation. Katie stood by the fire, because she was always cold, and the light glowed around her blond pigtails. Her little voice was clear and sure.

Now tears threatened in Jessie's eyes, and she forced herself to stop thinking about Katie. She scanned the seats for new absences. They might be important to remember, she told herself sternly.

Sadly, there were plenty to notice. Miranda Simpson was gone now, too, and Harlan Brill, Letitia Wittingham, James Benton, and Malcolm Steele. There were almost as many children missing as present.

Jessie wondered what excuse tourists got if they noticed all the absent pupils. Wait—she didn't have to wonder. Everyone thought she was a tourist. She might as well play along.

"Why are there so many empty seats?" she asked when Mrs. Spurning paused and seemed ready for questions. Jessie kept her voice innocent, the way she did when she teased Hannah.

"Oh, they're having some germs going around. Colds, nothing serious. I'm sure there are times when Oakdale's a little empty, too," Mrs. Spurning said.

Her tone was so casual that Jessie decided Mrs. Spurning really believed what she said. How was she to know?

"Shh," Mrs. Spurning said. "It's time for the seventh and eighth graders. Would you all know this?"

In unison, Mary, Hannah, Chester, and Richard began reeling off the states and the years they had joined the union. They stumbled a little between Tennessee and Ohio (1796 and 1803), but the students around Jessie looked impressed.

"They don't have as many to memorize," one boy said.

"True. But could you do even half?"

The boy grinned and shook his head. Jessie wasn't quite sure what Mrs. Spurning meant—how many states did the United States have? And why didn't these children know them? But Jessie liked Mrs. Spurning defending her friends.

Mary looked right out at them just then, and Jessie had to fight back the impulse to yell out, "Mary, I'm right here." Mary looked sad and her braids drooped. Jessie would have liked to have told her that Jessie, at least, wasn't sick.

The other children around Jessie were getting restless, as though it were them sitting on the school benches. They whispered and laughed while Mrs. Spurning talked on. If anyone in Clifton's school had done that, Mr. Smythe would have sent them to a corner or, worse, gotten out his whip. But Mrs. Spurning and the chaperon didn't scold anyone.

Mrs. Spurning just sighed, looked at a timepiece on her wrist, and said they should go.

This time Jessie would have liked to linger, watching her classmates recite under the stern gazes of Mr. Smythe and the George Washington and Martin Van Buren portraits. Here, finally, she was somewhere Mr. Smythe couldn't yell at her.

But Jessie followed the group out, and then down a different hall. This one had paintings, not those clear pictures-that-weren't-drawings. All the pictures had writing underneath, like, "1848. California Gold Rush," and "1876. Invention of the telephone." They led up to a mirror with the caption, "1996. You visit Clifton Village!"

Jessie realized the pictures were hints about what had happened in the one hundred and fifty years she thought of as the future. It might have been good to study them, but they made no sense to her. What was a telephone? One picture's caption said, "First airplane flight, 1903," and showed a man in a strange contraption apparently soaring through the sky. It had to be a fake. People couldn't fly. Or could they? Jessie's ignorance scared her. What if she couldn't make sense of anything in the outside world?

The pictures made Jessie so nervous, she decided to ignore them. In spite of her fear, she had to leave. The tour had already delayed her, and who could say what even a few hours meant to Katie and the others?

At the end of the hall, Mrs. Spurning said good-bye and left the children to the harried chaperon.

"All right, kids, you can eat your lunches now. If you brought money, you can go to the snack bar. Let's all sit in a group over there. Okay?" the chaperon said, pointing to the tables and chairs where the guards had sat the night before.

Jessie liked the chaperon a little better for saying "okay." So it was allowed out here!

"I'm going to the gift shop," Nicole said. "Want to come? I think they sell some of those horseshoes the blacksmith makes."

For a minute, Jessie was tempted. It would be less obvious if she went into whatever this gift shop place was, instead of walking out the door right away. She'd never seen a "gift shop" before. And maybe Nicole would tell her what it was like being a Negro. The only way Nicole seemed different was that she was nicer than the other children.

But Jessie remembered she didn't have time for curiosity.

"No thanks," she finally told Nicole. "I've got to find my, uh, classmates."

Jessie wished she hadn't had to lie to Nicole.

"Okay," Nicole said. "It was nice meeting you."

Jessie watched Nicole turn and walk away. Then, when the chaperon looked the other way, Jessie headed for the front door.

TEN

The world outside had a floor—not quite like the shiny floor inside the building, but solid gray, with lines every four feet or so. And wait—farther on, a little lower, part of the floor was solid black, and kind of tarry. Jessie had never seen anything like it. Who put floors outdoors?

Jessie was so busy looking at the ground that it took her a minute to notice the rows and rows of carriages—at least, they looked kind of like carriages—parked on some of the black floor. There must have been hundreds of them, some shiny red, some blue, others green or white. They gleamed in the sunshine. Jessie went closer to look at one. She heard a woman coaxing a little boy.

"Come on, Jason. Get out of the car," the woman said.

"Car," Jessie repeated under her breath. The word did sound like "carriage." So this was what Ma had been talking about when she said Miles Clifton had a limousine, and a limousine was a very big car. Were these limousines or just regular cars?

Whatever they were, Jessie decided they were grand. She watched one turn in to the driveway near her. It didn't have horses! How did it move?

Hoonk!

The noise sounded like the geese that came through Clifton in the fall and spring. Jessie turned around and saw the *hoonk* came from a car that had its nose pointed right at her. Inside, a woman sat behind a wheel looking mad.

Jessie jumped out of the way, then looked back as the car sped by. However these cars worked, it seemed they did something to the people in them. Why had the woman looked so mean? Jessie thought of the stories some of the other children in Clifton told about witchcraft. Was that how cars worked? But Jessie hadn't believed such stories before, and she didn't believe them now.

Once the car was gone, Jessie glanced down to see where she was standing. She was relieved to find she was on a patch of grass, beside a small maple tree. The grass was thicker than she was used to, but it still looked good. Whatever else had happened to the world, at least some things were familiar. The outdoor floor didn't go everywhere.

But there wasn't time to relax on the grass and think about that. Jessie saw a sign that said CLIFTON VILLAGE EXIT. Was it safe to just walk away from the tourists and all their cars? Casually, Jessie glanced around to make sure no one was watching. A few adults walked among the rows of cars, but none seemed to notice Jessie. Good. Two men were spraying water on a startling bunch of flowers near the door, but they were facing the opposite direction.

Feeling more confident, Jessie began walking toward the exit sign. She marveled that Ma's plan seemed to be working: Evidently no one had noticed Jessie was gone. Mr. Seward and the others that Ma called "Clifton's men" must think she was sick in bed, like Katie. Otherwise—Jessie shivered. Otherwise there would probably be plenty of guards around, looking specifically for her. And as long as she stayed near the tourists, she'd be easy to find.

Jessie walked faster, grateful for the arrowed exit signs that appeared every fifty yards or so. But she stopped in her tracks when the arrows pointed her around a corner.

In front of her, lined up in diagonals, were about thirty enormous yellow cars—cars so big that Pa's blacksmith shop could have fit in any of them. Jessie gawked. Was this what Ma meant when she said limousines were big cars? Were these all Miles Clifton's limousines?

Jessie edged close enough to read the lettering on the side of each car: GRANT COUNTY SCHOOL DISTRICT, M.S.D. OF MARTINSVILLE, SCHOOL BUS. The lettering didn't tell Jessie if the big cars were limousines or not, but she did recognize the word *school*. These must not belong to Miles Clifton. Did the schoolchildren who were tourists at Clifton Village get to ride on those? Jessie felt a stab of envy for those future—what had the chaperon called them?—teenagers.

It was all Jessie could do to resist peeking in one of the windows of the school maybe-limousines. Later, she told herself. After she got help for Katie and the others, she could come back and look closely at them. But just in case—as she walked on, Jessie stared back to try and register all the details, so she could impress Andrew later. He'd be mad, any-how, that Jessie had gotten to leave Clifton and he hadn't.

Just beyond the cars and the school maybe-limousines, one more exit sign pointed down a road that disappeared into the forest. The road was wide and smooth, covered with more of the black tarry surface. It made the new road they'd just built into Clifton look ridiculously bumpy. But this road was lined with familiar split rail fences, just like the ones that sur-rounded animal pens in Clifton.

Jessie climbed the fence and walked by the trees, hiding whenever she heard a car go by. Sure, no one seemed to be looking for her, but she didn't want to take any chances. Besides, she didn't want any more cars *hoonk*ing at her.

Stumbling over roots and branches, Jessie realized she could go a lot faster on the smooth road. No, be cautious, she told herself. That wasn't like her. Hannah was the cautious one in the family. But Hannah wouldn't have been brave enough to leave Clifton. Jessie would just have to pretend she had Hannah's caution and her own bravery.

A twig snapped nearby and Jessie froze. Then she relaxed, hearing a squirrel chatter by an oak ahead of her. Jessie tried to remember what Ma had said about getting down to the main road:

"It will be a long walk, maybe a mile. If I remember the way they planned it, the road will wind around a lot. And then you'll see a highway"—Jessie had looked puzzled at that—"a very big road, bigger than anything you've ever seen before. There should be signs with numbers, only I can't remember. . . . Seventeen? Twenty-seven? Thirty-seven? I think it's a number like that. Turn north and walk along the road. It goes all the way to Indianapolis, but you should be able to find a phone long before you get there."

A robin chirped in one of the elms and Jessie smiled. If she had a mile or more to walk, she wasn't going to walk the whole way fretting. She didn't need to be as big a worrywart as Hannah! She should be happy to find out they still had robins and squirrels in the 1990s. Then she laughed at herself. Of course they would! It was hard not to think of this as the future, this strange new world she'd just found out about.

Feeling freer with her laughter, Jessie took longer steps. She could do that in pants. She'd always wondered what it would be like to be a boy. This was as close as she'd get.

All the boys back in Clifton, Jessie thought, would be jealous that Jessie was out in the woods instead of in school listening to Mr. Smythe yell. On nice spring days like this, Andrew and his friends began talking of playing hooky from school and going fishing in Crooked Creek. Of course Andrew never did, because he knew Pa would tan his hide. But some of the other boys' fathers actually let them. Jessie remembered Mr. Wittingham saying it didn't matter, as soon as Horace learned his figuring and a little reading, he was taking him out of school, anyhow.

"What's he need with all those names and dates? He's going to be a barrel maker the rest of his life, same as me!"

Andrew had tried the same excuse on Pa, but Pa would have none of it.

"Doesn't matter if you're a blacksmith forever or not. Your ma thinks there's a value in being educated just for the sake of being educated. She's probably right—and anyhow, you do what your ma wants," he'd said.

Now a new thought struck Jessie. Could Pa and Mr. Wittingham have said those things just to play a role for the tourists? What if they didn't believe their own words? What did they really think?

It was too confusing—and scary—to ponder. Jessie went back to studying the landscape around her. Except for the road to her right and the long line of split rail fences, it looked just like the woods surrounding Clifton.

Jessie heard a car behind her and stepped behind a huge evergreen until it passed on. The noise zoomed by, but then it seemed to slow down. From the sound, Jessie guessed that the car had almost stopped, maybe one hundred yards down the road. Then the noise picked up again and faded away.

Jessie crept from behind the tree, scratching her face on the tree's needles. She crouched beside the rail fence and looked down the road. There was a small building ahead, like the guardhouses or sentry stations that surrounded all the forts in Jessie's history book pictures. The car must have slowed down passing the guardhouse. Well, she'd just have to go deeper into the woods and circle around the guard. Then she'd find her way back to the road—and to that main road with the number name—as soon as she passed the guardhouse.

Proud that she'd thought to stay off the road all along, Jessie crawled back to the evergreen. She was sure the guard had not seen her. Even if he'd been looking her way, she would have been hidden by the fence and the trees.

Now it wouldn't be long, Jessie told herself. She moved deeper into the woods. The underbrush was denser here, and she had to shove branches and vines out of her way. She didn't care. She was almost away from Clifton, and maybe it wouldn't be far down that number-name road before she'd find the thing Ma called a phone. . . .

Then Jessie saw the fence.

It was huge, at least twice Jessie's height, maybe three times. It was made of some kind of metal. Even yards away, Jessie could see the intricate twists of strong metal that would take Pa years to make. And at the top, almost at a right angle from the rest of the fence, there were rows of wires full of poking barbs. Those would be sharp, Jessie realized numbly. She could probably climb the fence, but she was bound to tear her clothes. And what if—? Oh no.

It took Jessie only a minute to recognize the box high up in an oak by the fence. It moved without wind. Yet, unlike the one she'd seen in the haunted tree all those years ago—the one she'd been spanked for seeing—no one had bothered to paint this box the same color as bark.

It was the thing Ma called a camera.

That was why there hadn't been more guards among the tourists up by Clifton. Miles Clifton wasn't worried about any Clifton resident getting this far. They couldn't climb the fence without being seen.

Jessie hadn't really understood Ma's explanation of cameras, but she knew that if she started climbing the fence, guards would probably arrive even before she reached the sharp points at the top. And Jessie felt sure this wasn't the only camera. If almost every inch of Clifton was watched, so was every inch of this fence. Jessie moved forward—yes, several trees down, on the other side, another box moved soundlessly.

And its glass eye was moving right toward her.

ELEVEN

Jessie ducked under a tree branch, but she knew it was hopeless. She couldn't hide well enough in time. And then—the camera stopped moving, just short of the point where it would see Jessie. It jerked back in the other direction, stopped there, and began flowing toward Jessie again.

Jessie crashed back through the underbrush and collapsed, clear out of sight, behind the wide trunk of an oak. Her heart pounded for a long time. She could feel the beating in her ears.

Peeking back at the cameras, she figured it out: They only looked at the fence. Each one must have a small section of fence to spy on, and they turned back and forth all day, just gazing at that one length of fence.

Jessie was thinking of the cameras as being alive, like animals smart enough to be tattletales and dumb enough to spend their entire lives in one tree. Probably that wasn't the right way to think about it, but she wasn't sure she could understand anything else. How could anything see if it wasn't alive?

That's enough, Jessie told herself. She was getting scared thinking of half-alive things. That wasn't the most important question, anyhow. She needed to think about how to get past the fence and the cameras without being seen.

Frustrated, Jessie picked at a dead piece of bark. She could walk along the fence, to see if it went all the way around Clifton. Even if it did, there might be an area the cameras didn't look at. If the cameras missed the King of the Mountain rock in Clifton, maybe outside . . .

Jessie's hopes rose for a moment, then she realized how stupid her plan was. It could take days to walk the perimeter of the fence. During that time, Katie and the others might— Jessie tried not to think the frightening word. It came anyway. *Die.*

Jessie threw the dead bark into the underbrush, as if that could take away the thought. Her heart started beating faster again.

I can't get over that fence without being seen, she thought. There's no way. I can't help Katie and the others. Ma was wrong to think I could. Oh, please, God, what am I supposed to do?

Jessie didn't realize she was praying—Reverend Holloway certainly never would have approved of her plea. It lacked even a single "thee" or "thou." She wondered, strangely, if God had any connection with the world outside Clifton.

But something calmed her. She suddenly had the feeling there was a way out, if only she could think of it.

Think about it as a problem in school, she told herself. Or no—a riddle. Nathan and Bartholomew had gone through a phase where one of them had a new riddle every day. Jessie had no idea where they heard them. The riddles always sounded ridiculous, nonsensical, as though they could have no right answer. Then you heard the answer and thought, Oh. That makes sense. It's stupid but it makes sense. Jessie remembered hearing Pa play along with one of the riddles not long ago.

"What eats as long as it lives, but dies as soon as it drinks?" Nathan had asked, carrying wood into the smithy.

Pa paused while his iron heated in the fire.

"Let me get this straight. Any drink kills it? Even water?"

Nathan giggled. "Oh yes. Water most of all!"

Pa shook his head. "Can't be such a thing. Anything alive needs water as much as it needs food. More, even."

"Not fire! It's fire!" Nathan's shrill voice exploded with laughter, though Pa was at least the tenth person he'd told the riddle to.

Pa pretended to study the flames in front of him.

"Well, I reckon you tricked me on that one. I'm not sure it's fair calling fire alive, but you're right, this fire will eat anything. And as soon as I pour water on it, it's out. I must be pretty dumb, not knowing that with the answer right in front of me."

Pa hung his head in mock shame. Then the iron reached the right shade of red orange and he pulled it out and began pounding. He moved skillfully, keeping the rhythm even as he grinned at Nathan.

Now Jessie bit her lip, wishing she hadn't conjured up

such a memory. She didn't have time to miss Pa and Nathan and the rest of her family. She had to get past the fence.

Distantly, she heard the drone of another car moving along the road from Clifton. Something clicked. As far as she knew, the fence had only one break, by the guardhouse. There was a human guard there, not a camera. Maybe . . .

Without a firm plan, Jessie moved through the underbrush toward the guardhouse. She crept slowly, trying not to rustle the bushes. She'd always heard Indians were good at walking through the woods without making a sound, but it wasn't a skill she'd learned. The guard didn't turn around, though, and the cars were going by too fast for anyone in them to notice.

Finally Jessie reached a bush opposite the guardhouse. She was close enough to see the hair on the back of the guard's neck. It was black and bristly. He was wearing a loose-fitting shirt, suspenders, and britches just like Pa wore, but Jessie knew that didn't mean he was from Clifton. It was like Mrs. Spurning wearing a long skirt; Mrs. Spurning and this man both looked a little uncomfortable in their clothes.

Another car pulled up. The guard turned to the driver, and Jessie ducked lower in the bush.

"Welcome to Clifton!" the guard said. "Parking's at the top of the hill. The ticket window's right inside the front door of the guest center. Tours are available every thirty minutes, on the hour and half hour."

An arm reached out from the car and seemed to be giving the guard money. Jessie wasn't sure what that was for. Did people actually pay to watch Clifton? Jessie gasped.

"That's quite a fence you have there," a man's voice

growled. "I was afraid I'd turned into the state prison by mistake."

Jessie saw the guard look toward the fence. She listened intently to his answer.

"Oh, our fence isn't that big," the guard said. "It's just that we have something of a game preserve around Clifton— the same number of bears, wolves, deer, you know, that would have been here in the 1800s. There's no danger, but some of Clifton's neighbors are farmers with livestock and they're happier with a fence between us."

Jessie waited for the man in the car to say that was ridiculous. Everyone knew there were bears and wolves and deer everywhere. Weren't there? The man only grunted.

"Look, Jamey. See the man's funny costume?" a woman's voice said from the car.

That bothered Jessie. She couldn't see the woman or Jamey, but she'd bet anything they had on stranger costumes than the guard's ordinary clothes.

Then the car drove on and Jessie returned to studying her escape route. The guard seemed occupied in his booth, so she risked moving to another bush with a better view.

The road split into two here, with the guardhouse in the middle. A long thin rail hung about three feet off the ground, reaching from the guardhouse almost to the bushes by Jessie. As two more cars drove up, Jessie watched the process. People would pay, the rail would lift magically, by itself, then it lowered again as soon as the car was past.

Jessie thought about witchcraft again, and pushed the thought away. Probably there was a pulley involved, or something like that. The inside of the Clifton mill would look like magic, too, if you didn't know how much water turned the wheel outside. Still, Jessie didn't like the moving rail.

She waited for a car to leave, most curious about what happened then. Finally a big yellow one—one of the monster maybe-limousines Jessie had gawked at earlier—roared down the road. It was packed with schoolchildren now. It slowed down, almost stopping. The driver seemed to be easing it over some large bump. Then it sped up and disappeared. Evidently, there was no rail to stop people on the way out.

Jessie frowned. That meant she couldn't hide in a car while it stopped for the rail. Well, she still had another option. She could hike back up the hill, hide in one of the empty cars, and wait for it to leave.

If that was her plan, she needed to start walking. But something made Jessie stay near the guardhouse. She'd lose so much time walking all the way back up the hill. Then what if she hid in a car that didn't leave for hours and hours? She could lose a whole day, a day that could make a lot of difference to Katie and the others.

Impatient with herself, Jessie watched several more cars come and go. Why? How was she going to get a better plan? She promised herself: I'll start walking after the next car goes by. Then it would disappear. One more, she thought. And then, one more.

Finally a different kind of vehicle came down the hill. It was bigger than most of the cars Jessie had seen, but not quite as big as the maybe-limousines the schoolchildren rode in. On the side, it carried a picture of sliced bread and the label FLAVORBEST.

FlavorBest? Jessie thought. Was that even a word? Thinking hard, Jessie watched the bread car slow down, like all the others had done before they passed the guardhouse.

Then—it stopped.

The vehicle still rumbled, as though it could jump forward at any minute. It reminded Jessie of horses that constantly pawed the ground when you made them stop. You knew they'd rather gallop on. But the vehicle didn't move. A man stepped out from the left side and walked to the guardhouse.

"How about those Reds?" the bread man asked.

"Oh yeah! Two on base, and then—"

They might as well have been speaking a foreign language, as much sense as it made. Jessie listened only to make sure they kept talking. This was her chance. The bread man was blocked by the wall of the guardhouse. The guard faced away from Jessie. Jessie gripped her pack and dashed out from the bushes.

Jessie's feet only touched ground six times, and she ran doubled over, but she felt like she was in open view for hours. Finally she reached the back of the guardhouse and crouched again. She listened hard, heart thumping.

"Seven errors!" the guard was saying. "Seven!"

"But in the fifth inning—"

Jessie tuned them out again. They hadn't seen her. That was all that mattered.

The door nearest Jessie was in full view of the two men, so Jessie decided to circle the vehicle and go in the other side. She reached the back of the vehicle, and paused to look for cameras before she went on.

"Unit ten, unit ten, what's your location?"

The voice came from inside the vehicle. Jessie froze.

"There's that SOB I was telling you about," the bread man said. "We never needed radios before and now he has to know where we are every single second—"

His voice got louder. He was walking back toward Jessie.

Jessie's knees shook. She should dive back into the bushes. But she was so close!

A knob on the back of the vehicle dug into her back. She shifted slightly and realized it was some sort of lever. Maybe, maybe . . .

Recklessly, Jessie jerked the lever this way and that. Finally it gave way, and a door opened into the back of the car. She saw racks loaded with bright loaf-shaped packages, but no man. Without allowing herself to wonder where the "unit ten, unit ten" voice had come from, she slipped in the door and pulled it almost closed behind her. It didn't latch.

Seconds later, the voice came again.

"Unit ten, unit ten—are you in your truck?"

Just then, the bread man climbed in the front and picked up a small black square.

"Unit ten to base, unit ten to base. I'm in my truck. I'm leaving Clifton Village right now."

So this kind of vehicle was called a truck, Jessie thought. But what was that voice?

"You were supposed to be at North Elementary twenty minutes ago." The crackly voice seemed to come from nowhere.

"It's not my fault. I've told you how slow these people out here are," the bread man said into the box.

In spite of her awe at the mysterious voice, Jessie almost

giggled. The bread man sounded as whiny as Chester Seward when Mr. Smythe scolded him for forgetting his books: "It's not my fault. My sister's supposed to carry them."

The bread man put the black box down, said a few words Jessie thought must be bad even in the 1990s, and shoved a stick by his chair.

The vehicle lurched forward. Jessie peeked out and saw the fence slide past. One of the camera-boxes jerked toward the truck, but Jessie yanked the door shut—in time, she thought. She waited, clutching the door, but nobody screamed for the truck to stop. No guards came running. The truck was going too fast for anyone to catch it, anyhow.

Jessie had escaped Clifton.

The vehicle gathered speed. Wind blew violently back toward Jessie, rattling the wrappers on the racks of bread. It was all she could do to hold on to the unlatched door. She was sure she'd never been in anything moving this fast in her life—well, not that she could remember.

The vehicle went still faster. Jessie's rejoicing turned a little sour. She'd escaped Clifton. How was she going to escape this wild bread truck?

TWELVE

Jessie braced herself between a bread rack and the door. Every few seconds, she would think the vehicle couldn't possibly go any faster. Then it would make a gravelly noise— like some dying animal gasping for air—and speed up. With each burst of speed, Jessie's stomach churned and the bread racks shook harder. Jessie remembered what Mr. Wittingham said every time Clifton heard of some new invention: "Ain't natural." Well, going this fast wasn't natural, and Jessie wasn't sure she liked it.

In the front, the bread man was singing as carelessly as someone might sing strolling through Clifton. It even sounded to Jessie as if he had others singing with him, and a musical instrument or two. She had to be imagining that, though.

Jessie shifted her grip on the unlatched side of the door.

Caught suddenly in a powerful wind, it swung open.

"What the—" the bread man in the front swore. He hit the brakes, and they worked better than the brakes of any carriage Jessie had ever been in. Jessie's body slammed against the latched half of the truck's back end. A metal rack toppled against her. Some of the brightly packaged loaves of bread flew out the open door.

Strangely, the music continued.

Jessie crouched, waiting for the bread man to turn around and see her. How could she explain? Would he force her to go back to Clifton? Would he call Miles Clifton and his men? She'd have to try to outrun him. But could she run at all after being hit by the bread racks?

Jessie flexed her arms and legs, just a little, and decided nothing was broken. She'd probably end up with lots of bruises. But that was the least of her worries.

The bread truck shuddered to a stop. A last loaf toppled on Jessie's head. Peering through the crooked racks, Jessie saw the bread man step out his door.

Jessie had a moment of panic—he was going to find her!—then she grabbed her pack and jumped out the back door. Immediately, she spun around the side of the truck opposite the bread man. Maybe he wouldn't see her. . . . An open ditch sloped before Jessie and she rolled into its tall grasses.

Jessie peeked from the grasses in time to see the bread man come around the other side of the truck. He picked up a squished package of bread and then threw it down in disgust.

"How'm I going to explain this?" he complained. "I'm going to be even later and I won't have enough bread. . . .

They'll say I didn't latch the door, and I know I did."

He looked at the open door. Jessie ducked lower in the grass, afraid he'd start looking for someone else to blame.

"It's got to be broken," the bread man said.

He fiddled with the latch. Jessie heard it clicking.

"Normal," the bread man said, and swore.

Jessie began to tremble. She felt sorry for the bread man, but she couldn't pop up and explain the mysterious open door. He was already mad; he probably wouldn't even listen to her. He'd just take her back to Clifton. He might do that anyway if he found her. For all she knew, he might be one of "Clifton's men."

Jessie pressed closer to the ground, as if that would make her invisible. She heard the bread man slam the door of the truck. He swore some more. Was he coming to look for her?

Then she heard another vehicle pull up behind the bread truck. Peeking through the grasses, Jessie saw a red car.

"Can I help? What happened?" a man's voice said.

"Door broke," the bread man said.

Jessie heard a car door slam. The second man seemed to be looking around. What if he was looking for her?

She risked another glance—she should know if she'd have to run—but both men were staring at the back of the truck.

"Want help picking up the bread?" the second man said.

"Nah. Forget it," the bread man said in disgust. "It's no good now."

Then both men got into their vehicles and drove away.

Jessie waited in the ditch for a while, in case one of them figured out what happened and came back to look for her. But if they did—shouldn't she be as far away as possible?

Staying as low in the ditch as she could, she crept forward.

Jessie wasn't sure how long she half crawled, half slithered through the ditch. The knees of her pants got wet and muddy. Her muscles began to ache from the unusual position, and she decided she was being silly. Anyone looking for her would have reached this spot already. Those cars went so fast she wasn't going to beat them by crawling. Besides, she needed to know if she was crawling in the right direction.

Jessie stood up.

In front of her, two wide roads spread from horizon to horizon. It was the widest clearing Jessie had ever seen in her life. The widest one she remembered, at least. Even beyond the roads there were no woods, only a few trees scattered in pastures or beside houses. Jessie felt her throat catch at the unfamiliar sight. What had happened to all the trees? Sure, settlers were clearing space for farms and villages, but Mr. Smythe had said a squirrel could cross Indiana jumping from tree to tree without once touching the ground, if he wanted to. Were the woods around Clifton the only ones left now?

A car whizzed by, and Jessie remembered she didn't have time to mourn the woods. She needed to find out if she was on the right road, going the right way. An enormous truck thundered by with a force that flattened the grasses by the road and whipped Jessie's hair into her face. Even if walking was slower, Jessie was glad to be out of the bread truck.

After a few moments of watching, Jessie noticed the cars traveled in different directions on the different roads. On the road by Jessie, the cars went—Jessie glanced at the sun. It was too high overhead to be sure of direction. How could she find out?

Then she saw a sign several feet ahead. She ran toward it. The sign came into focus: 37. That was one of the numbers Ma had said might be the right road. Above the number, the sign said NORTH. Jessie grinned. She was going toward Indianapolis.

Jessie touched the sign for good luck, amazed once again by the smoothness of the outside world's metal. She'd lost time escaping from Clifton and then the bread truck, but she was going in the right direction and she was bound to find one of those phone things soon. No one seemed to be looking for her. Surely the most frightening part of her journey was over.

Jessie slung her pack over her shoulder and began walking north. She started out in the ditch, but the ground was uneven and the grasses tore at her legs. Carelessly, forgetting the caution she'd pretended to borrow from Hannah, Jessie moved up the slope to a place where the walking was easier—and she was in plain sight of every car that passed.

THIRTEEN

M a had said it would probably be a couple miles before Jessie found a phone. As she walked, Jessie looked around anxiously. What if she passed all the phones because she didn't know what they looked like? But there was little on either side of the big road but grass and fields and an occasional tree. Jessie thought about asking someone, but the only people she saw were those zooming by in the fast cars. She wouldn't want to try to stop them.

Well, Jessie told herself with forced cheer, if they didn't stop, at least that meant they didn't want to capture her and take her back to Clifton.

Jessie's stomach gurgled just then, and she remembered that she hadn't eaten anything since—she wasn't sure. Was it lunch yesterday? When she ate just like usual in the school yard with Mary? As if impatient for Jessie to remember, her stomach rumbled again, louder.

Would it be wrong to stop and eat before finding one of the phone things? Now that she was safely outside Clifton, Jessie decided a short break wouldn't matter. She walked a ways, looking for a place to sit down. Then she saw a sign that said CROOKED CREEK and knew she'd found it.

Crooked Creek ran through Clifton, joining the White River right by the mill. Jessie felt sure this was the same winding creek she and Andrew had skipped stones in downriver. It made her feel good to crawl down along a bank where the water flowed toward Clifton. She dropped a twig in.

"Tell Ma I'm all right. No—say 'okay.' That way she'll know I'm outside," Jessie told the twig as it drifted by. She made a face at her own foolishness. Well, she couldn't help it. It was a little lonely out here. She'd never been alone for so long in all her life. And she'd never eaten a meal all by herself. She wasn't sure she could chew without Nathan screaming for the jam or Mary offering to trade lunches.

Jessie sat down on a flat rock by the creek and opened the pack Ma had given her. She had not had time to look before, but now she saw Ma had provided well. There were two loaves of bread—firm and pungent, not like that squishy stuff in the truck. That was something else weird about the bread truck, Jessie realized: The bread had had no smell. Jessie shrugged and pulled out one of the cloth-wrapped loaves. She saw Ma had also packed beef jerky and some of her anise cookies, Jessie's favorite.

Jessie had one of the cookies first—who was here to tell her not to?—and sorted through the pack to make sure she hadn't missed anything. Under the jerky was a strange container made of something like leather. Jessie would have said the container was a man's purse, if it hadn't had all the compartments.

At the back were some strips of paper. These had to be money, Jessie decided. She hoped it was still good. With so many banks failing, Mr. Seward was getting finicky about what money he would accept at the store. Most people in Clifton used coins or barter anyway. But Jessie might need to find someone to accept these bills outside Clifton. . . . Jessie pulled out one of the bills that said "20" on every end. It didn't have a bank name on it, only "Federal Reserve Note, The United States of America." And—a picture of Andrew Jackson! He looked just like he did in the portrait at home in Clifton.

Jessie forgot her worries over whether the money was any good or not. She was so happy to see a familiar face that she kissed President Jackson's picture. She giggled. Imagine if she met President Jackson in person and kissed him like that! Then she remembered: If it was really more than 150 years later than she thought, Andrew Jackson had died a long time ago. Even the bank problems all the men in Clifton complained about had happened 150 years ago. Maybe there were no money problems now. Maybe there were more.

Jessie's grin faded. She concentrated on counting the money, three more twenties and a couple that said "1," with George Washington's face on the front. At least President Washington's picture was familiar, too. Things couldn't be too different in the 1990s if people kept George Washington and Andrew Jackson on their money. Pa would be happy to know President Jackson was worth more.

"He may have won the Revolutionary War, but he was still

a Federalist," Pa always said about President Washington. Pa didn't think too highly of Federalists.

But Jessie was confused again. Pa already knew that Andrew Jackson was on a bigger bill than George Washington. Pa and Ma both had used this kind of money before they moved to Clifton.

Jessie rubbed her forehead. If only she could get everything straight in her mind. She took the last bill out, and a slip of paper fell to the ground. Jessie grabbed it before it blew into the creek. She unfolded the corners.

> *Jessie,*
> *By now you should know what I've told you is true. And maybe you've found some explanations for what I don't understand. . . . Know that in spite of everything, Pa and I love you. We never expected or wanted Clifton to turn out the way it did.*
> *There should be more than enough money and food here for you. Take care. I'll pray for you the whole time you're away.*
> *Ma*

At the bottom was the name "Isaac Neeley"—the man Jessie was supposed to tell about the illness—with the number for her to call when she found a phone. Ma had also written out instructions about what Jessie was supposed to say. But Jessie's eyes blurred too much to read that part. Suddenly she felt unbearably homesick for Ma's familiar writing and Pa's political comments and—yes, even Nathan's screaming for jam at breakfast. Well, she'd be back home again soon, as soon as she found a phone and got help for Katie and the others. And she could be brave until then.

Jessie put the note back in the area with the paper money and opened other compartments.

Coins spilled out of one spot, and Jessie almost knocked the whole pack into the water trying to retrieve them. It was one of these that Jessie would have to put in the phone, when she found one. But Ma hadn't been able to tell Jessie what coins to use.

"It's been so long," Ma had murmured. "And things might have changed. . . ."

Her voice had scared Jessie. Jessie tried not to think about it. She pried open another part of the billfold. This had pages, with papers stuck between a slippery surface.

"Pennsylvania Driver's License," the first paper said. It had another one of those picture-things that were too realistic to be drawings. She realized the picture was of Ma before she moved to Clifton.

Ma's light brown hair mostly went to her shoulders, with some of it cut shorter and curled. Jessie couldn't help thinking it was kind of ugly that way. But Ma's blue eyes were kind, as usual, and she was smiling gently, as though gazing at Pa. She looked as young as Hannah.

Jessie turned to the next page and saw another picture-thing, this time showing a baby and a little girl in a short dress.

"Hannah and Jessie, 1983," it said on the back.

This was proof, then, that Jessie had lived in the world outside Clifton.

Jessie felt so strange, she snapped the billfold shut and put it back in the pack. She tore off some of the bread and jerky and began eating, automatically.

All her life until today, if someone had asked Jessie who she was, she'd have had an easy answer: "I'm Jessie Keyser. My pa's the blacksmith here in Clifton, and I've lived here as long as I can remember. We came out from Pennsylvania. . . ."

But there had been no need for Jessie to tell anyone that, because everyone in Clifton knew her.

Now that Jessie knew Clifton wasn't a normal village, and it wasn't really 1840, did she know who she was? Could she go back to Clifton after this and live as she always had?

Jessie swallowed a bite of bread and it stuck in her throat. She bent over and cupped her hands in the creek, preparing to take a drink.

Then she heard yelling.

"Stop! Stop it!"

FOURTEEN

When Jessie dared to turn around, she saw a man bounding toward her. He had a grizzly gray beard and snapping eyes. He was also the fattest man Jessie had ever seen. Jessie thought she could outrun him if she had to, but it scared her that she hadn't known he was behind her. What if he were from Clifton?

"Stop!" he yelled again.

Panting, the man leaned on the fence right behind Jessie. Jessie braced to run if he climbed the fence. She was not going to let someone fatter than Mr. Seward catch her.

"I don't mind you trespassing on my land," the man said, "as long as you don't leave a mess. But I can't believe you'd be stupid enough to drink that water. Don't you know how many pesticides and herbicides flow into that creek every spring?"

Jessie wanted to act like a normal 1996 teenager, but she didn't know if she was supposed to say yes or no. So she said nothing.

Glaring, the man said, "You really don't, do you? I mean, it's poison! Stupid city kid."

Jessie let the water spill through her fingers. Poison? It didn't look any different from the well water at home. No one drank out of Crooked Creek in Clifton, but Jessie had thought that was just because everyone had wells.

"I'm sorry," she said. "Where can I get a drink that isn't, uh, poison?"

She looked down at the water again. It sparkled in the sunlight filtered through the bushes. Poison? The man was probably crazy.

"There's a million gas stations with stores on 37," the man said. "For all the Clifton Village tourists. People have to get their last fix of the twentieth century before they risk seeing the past."

The man's voice was sarcastic. Jessie wondered if she dared ask what a gas station was. And what did people fix in the stores?

"So they would have water at the . . . gas stations?" she finally asked, hoping it wasn't a giveaway question.

"Sure, water, pop, juice, beer, you name it. They'll sell you anything. It's a capitalist age we live in, my dear." Jessie decided to ask the more important question.

"Would they have a phone?"

"Sure," the man said. He paused. "Oh, just come on up to my house and I'll get you a glass of water. Free. You can use the phone, too, as long as it's a local call. It won't be the first time my afternoon walk's interrupted. It's not like I care that much about losing weight. It's for my wife. She keeps asking, 'Isn't there something hypocritical about being a fat environmentalist? Using up all the world's resources?'"

The man gestured for Jessie to climb the fence and follow him.

Jessie hesitated. The man didn't sound like he worked for Miles Clifton. He seemed a little crazy, but not dangerous. He'd called himself an environmentalist, which was a word Ma had used. Maybe it was all right to go with him. Yet Ma had warned Jessie to be wary of all strangers, not just Clifton's guards.

"That was one reason Pa and I wanted to raise you children in Clifton," Ma had said. "We didn't want to terrify you into staying away from strangers. It's odd—all the time, you were in danger here. And now all of you are too trusting. People in the outside world . . ."

Ma hadn't finished the thought, which scared Jessie plenty.

"No, that's all right. I'll go to the, um, gas station," Jessie told the man now.

The man looked at her curiously.

"You're a little young to be out on your own, aren't you? Do your parents know where you are?"

"Oh yes," Jessie said. It wasn't a total lie. One of her parents knew what she was doing, anyway. "In fact, I'm on an errand for my mother. I should be going now."

The man looked at her doubtfully, but he shook his head. "Guess it's none of my business."

Jessie scrambled to her feet and stuffed the remains of her lunch back in the pack. She walked across the bridge and then along the big road, feeling the man's eyes on her back. The memory of Ma's warning spooked her. What might the man do? What had Ma been warning her against? Even though the man seemed nice, would he report her to Miles Clifton?

Jessie was glad when the road dipped and she was out of the man's sight. She wondered if all conversations with strangers were so strange. Until leaving Clifton, she'd never talked to anyone she hadn't known for a long time. And now she had trouble making sense of everyone: the guards, the teenage tourists, Mrs. Spurning and the chaperon, the bread man, and now the fat environmentalist. Was Jessie stupid, or was everyone outside Clifton crazy? Was that maybe why Jessie's parents and the other families had wanted to move to Clifton? Or did the people she'd met seem strange just because she didn't know them, and didn't understand the twentieth century?

Jessie couldn't figure any of it out. She was getting so thirsty she could barely think. She decided to try to look for a gas station, since it would have both a phone and a drink. But, again, she didn't know what she was looking for.

Then, about a mile beyond Crooked Creek, she saw a sign on a tall post, with the words THE STOPPING POINT. Underneath, it said GAS, LIVE BAIT, PIZZA, COOL DRINKS. Beneath the sign, there was a small white building and strange contraptions that looked like hitching posts for cars. At least, people would drive up to them and loop a hose to the car, like someone in Clifton would tie a horse's reins to a hitching post. But not all the cars had to be hitched like that—others were just parked by the store.

It didn't make sense, but Jessie didn't care. This had to be a gas station!

Jessie dodged the cars waiting for the hitching posts and pushed open the door of the store. At first, it seemed dim after the sunshine outside. Then Jessie's eyes adjusted and she realized the globe-things were almost as bright as the sun. Jessie felt a pang, missing the dim coolness of Mr. Seward's store. But it was easier to see in here, and she was fascinated by all the bright packages. Where Mr. Seward had barrels and tins to hunt through, this place had shelves full of cookies and crackers and things she didn't even recognize, all in containers covered with labels and pictures. She grinned at a row of bread loaves in red-and-yellow wrappers—the same kind as the bread truck she'd ridden in. But there were also loaves in a dozen other wrappers. And the bread was about the only familiar food. What was a Frito? she wondered. A Cheeto? A Dorito?

Jessie was tempted to buy a lot of things, just to see what they were. But habit was hard to break. In Clifton, no one spent money unless it was for something desperately needed. And Jessie needed only a drink and a phone.

Jessie decided it was okay to get a drink first, since she was a little scared of trying to use a phone.

She went to the back, where rows and rows of bottles leaned behind glass windows. Most of them said "Coke" or "Pepsi," and Jessie wondered what that could be. Both drinks looked like cough syrup. She settled on a bottle of something called "Papaya fruit drink." It was prettier.

Jessie opened the glass door and felt air as cold as winter. She slammed the door. How could it be? This wasn't an icehouse or even a springhouse. Cautiously, Jessie forced herself to open the door again and grab the bottle of juice. The glass was cold. Jessie was tempted to let the juice warm up before she drank it. Pa always said it wasn't right to drink something cold in warm weather. But—it might taste better this way.

As Jessie took the mysteriously cold bottle to the front to pay, she noticed two round mirrors in the corner. Were they like the mirrors in Clifton that people looked through? She didn't like all this watching.

The strange cooped-up cold and the mirrors unnerved her. But as she stepped up to pay for her drink, she forced herself to ask the boy behind the counter about a phone.

"Right outside," he said without looking up. "Don't know how you missed it."

"Thank you."

Jessie gave the boy one of the George Washington bills, and he took it as though he saw paper money every day. Well, that proved the one-dollar bills were good. Jessie was a little bothered that it had been so easy. Mr. Seward would have taken out his magnifying glass and checked the signature on the bill. Then he'd ask, in his dry pretentious voice, "Do you have your parents' permission to spend this?" Mr. Seward didn't believe in children doing anything without their parents' permission. Especially not girls.

But this boy was not much older than Jessie. She watched him hit buttons on a box, then count out change from a drawer that sprang out when he stepped back. The box would have intrigued her if she hadn't been so curious about the boy. He had hair shaved close to his head, and wore a black—what was it called? oh yes—T-shirt. The T-shirt was covered with strange symbols; the word MEGADETH screamed across the front. Jessie wanted to ask what Megadeth was, but it was probably something she would have known if she hadn't been from Clifton.

Outside, Jessie counted the change the boy had given her. Eleven cents! That couldn't be right. That meant the drink had cost eighty-nine cents. Pa would have to shoe eight horses to make that much money, and she'd just spent eighty-nine cents on some silly drink. Why, that would buy pounds and pounds of flour at Mr. Seward's store. . . . Jessie wanted to go back and tell the Megadeth boy there'd been some mistake. But maybe money wasn't the same here. She took a drink and the liquid was nice and sweet, as well as pleasantly cool. Yet somehow it was spoiled for her.

This time Jessie noticed a small blue sign that said TELE-PHONE. It was on a rectangular box mounted on a post beyond the car hitching posts. She walked over. The box had the words "Deposit 25 cents" at the top. Jessie looked through her coins until she found one that said "quarter dollar."

Jessie lifted the club-thing that Ma had said to put by her ear and mouth. What if she got it upside down? Would she still be able to hear? For a moment, Jessie just stood there feeling strange, but then she dropped her quarter in. The little cup at her ear gave off an annoying buzz. Jessie hoped that was a good sign. She took out the note Ma had given her, with Isaac Neeley's name and phone number, and began hitting the numbers.

With each button she pressed, the little cup at her ear gave off a tone. It was like music, she decided.

The phone gave off another tone, and Jessie waited. Then there was a click.

"Please dial 1 before this long-distance number," a woman's even voice said from the earpiece.

Jessie jumped. So you really could hear people talking on a phone! She pulled the earpiece away from her ear and looked at it suspiciously. The box and the earpiece were too small for a woman to be hiding inside. And Jessie could see that no one was talking on the other side of the box. How did the voice get in the phone?

Jessie was so surprised, she forgot what the woman had said.

"Hello?" Jessie said. "What did you say? Can I talk to Mr. Neeley?"

Jessie felt foolish talking into the phone. It was like talking to a book or a house or something else that wasn't alive. Jessie wasn't used to talking to anything but people. Had she done it right?

The voice didn't answer.

"Hello?" Jessie said again. "I just want to talk to Mr. Neeley. Can you please get him for me?"

She didn't know what else to say. Still, no one answered. Jessie wondered if the phone worked after all. Maybe she would have to walk all the way to Indianapolis to talk to Mr. Neeley. But at least someone had talked on the phone. . . . She heard something falling through the phone. Her coin?

Jessie took her quarter dollar out of a small door at the bottom. Maybe it was just a bad coin. That happened sometimes. There were counterfeiters around. Jessie had seen men test coins with their teeth to make sure they were real. Now that she noticed, this one didn't look like real silver.

Jessie tried another quarter and hit the buttons again. Again, she heard the odd music, the tone, and the click.

"Please dial 1 before this long-distance number," the woman said again.

"A 1?" Jessie said. "Why? I know it's a long distance. That's why I'm using the phone—"

Jessie had the feeling the woman wasn't listening to her. Her coin fell through the phone again.

Jessie put the quarter back in. She hit a 1 hesitantly, but nothing happened. She hit the numbers Ma had written out for her to call.

The odd music and clicks were almost familiar now. A new voice answered: "Please deposit one dollar and forty cents."

At least it was something new. Jessie pulled out the rest of her money. One dollar and forty cents was a fortune. But it made sense that it would be expensive to talk to someone forty miles away. Jessie counted out the right amount, then tried to figure out where to put the dollar in the phone.

"Where?" she asked. "Do you want me to fold up the dollar and put it where the quarter went? I'm afraid it will get stuck—"

No one answered.

"Hello?" Jessie said. "I want to give you the money, but I don't know where to put it."

No answer.

Jessie was worried. If Mr. Neeley stayed on the phone as briefly as everyone else, Jessie would never have a chance to explain about Katie and the others. But she started to fold up the dollar bill, to try to put it in the little quarter hole. In her haste, she knocked some of her coins to the ground. She bent over to pick them up. Seeing all the coins on the ground gave her an idea. She could put one dollar and forty cents in coins into the phone! Jessie felt really smart, until she hit her head on the bottom of the phone standing up. When she listened to the earpiece again, it made a nasty buzzing noise. Had she broken the phone?

Jessie hung the earpiece back on its cradle, and looked around nervously. Several cars were at the hitching posts, but no one seemed to be looking at her. Jessie picked up the earpiece again, put her quarter in, dialed the number with the 1 in front of it, then put one dollar and forty cents in coins in the hole when the voice asked for it.

The phone began ringing.

Jessie grinned. That was what Ma had said would happen!

Jessie cleared her throat, ready to talk. But the ringing continued. When was Mr. Neeley going to answer? The other voices had come out of the phone right away.

Jessie stopped grinning. She counted the rings. Eleven, twelve . . . twenty . . . twenty-five. . . . Still, no one answered. Jessie waited longer. The ringing began to hurt her ears.

Finally Jessie eased the phone back in its cradle. She tried to remember if Ma had said anything about this. Yes: "You may not reach Mr. Neeley at first. He may not be home to answer. If that happens, you'll have to wait and try again."

Slowly, Jessie put the phone's club-thing back in its cradle. She could wait if she had to. But could Katie and the other sick children?

FIFTEEN

Jessie stood next to the phone, trying to decide how long she should wait before dialing Mr. Neeley's number again. And then she felt the bump from behind. She half turned and saw a man slipping. His limbs jolted outward; his left arm brushed the note from Ma and knocked it to the ground. The force of his fall brought Jessie down, too.

"Oh, excuse me," the man said. "You aren't hurt, are you? I'm so clumsy. Looks like I haven't broken in this new pair of feet yet."

Jessie scrambled to her feet and looked at the man suspiciously. His fall reminded her of the way Chester Seward and Richard Dunlap sometimes acted during recess at school, knocking down girls "by accident" so they could look up the girls' skirts. But this man was an adult, and Jessie was wearing pants like a boy.

Then the man picked up Ma's note and looked at it.

No! Jessie wanted to scream. What if the man was from Clifton? Should she run? But she couldn't get help without Ma's note—

"This must be yours," the man said casually, handing the scrap of paper to Jessie. "I am so sorry. Are you done with the phone? That was really why I walked over here, not to put you in traction. You are all right, aren't you?"

"Y-yes," Jessie stammered, clutching the note.

The man turned away, took out a notebook from his jacket, and seemed to be writing something down. Then he picked up the phone.

Jessie backed away from the man, her thoughts jumbled. The man couldn't be from Clifton, because he would have captured her right there. Wouldn't he? But why had he knocked her down? Why had he looked at her note? What had he written?

Jessie wanted to believe the man had nothing to do with her or Clifton. Still, she couldn't shake her fear. Blindly, she turned and ran.

Risking one glance over her shoulder, Jessie saw that the man was still talking on the phone. She kept on. The man had acted so strangely and was dressed so strangely—he wore a blue shirt with an odd strip of flowered cloth hanging down from his neck. But everyone seemed odd to Jessie outside Clifton. . . .

Panting, Jessie slowed down. She couldn't run forever. And she had to keep looking for a phone. Now that she knew they had blue signs above them, she would surely find another one soon. And then she'd get help for Katie and the others, and she wouldn't have to worry anymore about whether the strange people she saw were or were not on Miles Clifton's side.

But Jessie walked miles without seeing another one of the blue phone signs. She wondered if she should have stayed by the phone at the Stopping Point, in spite of the strange man. She worried about the puzzle even Ma didn't understand— why did anyone want the children of Clifton to die of diphtheria? Mrs. Spurning, the guide for the tourists back at Clifton, had said Clifton residents got modern medical care, so the tourists must not care if Clifton was totally authentic. How could anyone want Katie—sweet little Katie—to die? Or Betsy Benton? Or any of the Clifton children?

Jessie blinked back tears and walked faster. She had to find a phone. When she got hungry again, she didn't stop, but pulled a hunk of bread out of her pack and ate while she walked. She paused only for a moment to gulp down the last of the papaya juice. It left a too-sweet taste in her mouth. She longed for ordinary water. But the fat environmentalist's warning about poison water made her leery of drinking from any of the streams she crossed. Anyhow, there wasn't time to stop.

Jessie passed woods almost as dense as those around Clifton, and felt slightly better because that meant the Clifton woods weren't the last in the world. After a few miles, though, the landscape flattened out, and there were no more trees or hills to remind her of home. Except for the ditches on each side of the big road, the land was almost perfectly level. Long fences marked off enormous fields. Jessie recognized small corn plants growing in even rows in one of the fields. She marveled at the farmer who could plant so much. Mr. Atkins, who had the biggest fields in Clifton, only planted twenty rows of corn each spring, and bragged about it. This field had hundreds. And then there was another field just like it.

People must work really hard out here, Jessie thought. She hated hoeing just the little field that Pa kept.

Jessie's legs felt rubbery, just like they did after a long day of hoeing corn. She was sure she'd been walking for hours. The sun was sinking low in the sky now. In Clifton, school would have been out long ago, and all the children in the village would be doing their chores. Jessie wondered if Hannah had to do Jessie's and Katie's chores as well as her own. Bet she was complaining!

Jessie grinned at the thought of Hannah having to do everything. But Hannah wouldn't be any good helping Ma on her sick rounds. Hannah didn't even like to hear someone sneeze. Ma would probably run herself ragged tonight trying to help all the sick children. But from what Ma had said, she couldn't do much. She was counting on Jessie to bring the cure.

Jessie looked around, frantically searching for one of the blue phone signs. What if she didn't find a phone and reach Mr. Neeley before dark? What if she had to walk all the way to Indianapolis?

To distract herself, Jessie tried to remember everything she knew about the state's capital. Reverend Holloway had been there, and sometimes talked about what a sinful place it was. It was founded on a lie, he said.

When he wasn't around, though, Pa and some of the other men in Clifton laughed about how the settlers near

Indianapolis had tricked the state. About fifteen years ago, not long before Clifton was founded, the state decided the capital should be in the middle of Indiana, not down by the Ohio River in Corydon. So the state officials sent scouts up, and the settlers around Indianapolis told the scouts what a great place Indianapolis was, because it was easily reached on the White River. Except—boats couldn't go that far up the White River. You could only get to Indianapolis by stage-coach, and everyone knew that was hard.

"Well, those settlers fooled the state, but now we're stuck with a capital that'll never amount to anything," Pa always said when the others laughed too hard.

Jessie tried to remember what else she'd heard. It seemed there wasn't anything in Indianapolis except the legislature building and a couple others. Maybe there were more now. Or—maybe there were fewer. Ma hadn't said whether Indianapolis was still the capital in 1996.

Jessie kept walking.

Soon she could tell from the angle of the setting sun that the road was turning more to the east. Was that a problem? Ma had said this road went all the way to Indianapolis, but that had been years ago and maybe they'd moved the road or—

Jessie rounded a curve and saw an odd set of lights hanging over the road. While she watched, a green light at the bottom went out, and was replaced by a yellow light above it. Then the yellow light went out and a red light came on. The cars that had breezed by Jessie screeched to a stop before the red light.

Jessie stared. Now, how did that work? There didn't seem to be anyone around to change the lights. Looking around curiously, Jessie saw a sight that made her forget the lights. Off to the left, just beyond the road, was a cluster of about thirty houses and other buildings.

Jessie must have walked farther than she thought. This had to be Indianapolis.

Jessie was so excited, she didn't see the brown car until it was almost beside her. It was going the wrong way, backward. A boy with greasy hair sprang out.

"Get in!" he yelled at Jessie.

SIXTEEN

Jessie was too stunned to do anything but stare. The boy had a gold loop in one ear and Jessie thought instantly of pirates. The car shook beside him. Jessie saw a gaping hole surrounded by rust at the bottom of one door. The car wasn't shiny like the ones she'd seen back at Clifton. But what if the boy worked for Miles Clifton? Or—she'd heard one man back at Clifton talk about a prison—Jessie could believe this boy had escaped from a prison.

"I don't, I mean—" Jessie tried to sound calm, but her voice shook.

The boy laughed at her confusion. So did the driver of the car. All Jessie could see of him was a leg covered in ripped blue jeans.

"Hear that, Tol?" the boy said. "We back half a mile down 37 to pick up this hitchhiker and she don't even say thanks. Where you going, sugar?"

Jessie had never heard of a "hitchhiker." And she had never been called "sugar" before. Both words were ugly the way he said them.

"I'm going to Indianapolis," Jessie said. "It's right up there, so I don't need a ride."

She gazed longingly at the cluster of buildings near the odd green-yellow-red light. Was that?—she thought she saw a blue sign outside one of the buildings. So even if she couldn't find Mr. Neeley's house, maybe she could find a phone. If only she could get away from these boys.

The boy cackled. Jessie calculated that he was too close—if she tried to run, he could grab her instantly.

"You think that's Indianapolis?" he asked, pointing at the village ahead.

"Isn't it?" Was he trying to trick her?

The boy doubled over with laughter.

"Can you believe it, Tol?" he said. "She thinks that's Indianapolis!" He turned back to Jessie. "What planet were you born on, sugar? Let me clue you in to some Earth info—that little dump over there is Waverly—how many people you think live in Waverly, Tol?"

"Fifty," came from inside the car.

"Okay, fifty," the first boy said with a smirk. "And, see, no skyscrapers—big, tall buildings, you know? Indianapolis is about fifteen miles thataway, as they say in the movies, and a million people live there, and they have lots of skyscrapers. But don't worry. We'll take you there. Now, get in!"

He reached for Jessie's wrist and she pulled back. Maybe Indianapolis was still fifteen miles away. But there was no way she was getting in the car.

The boy lurched unsteadily toward her, and Jessie stepped back again. Despite her fright, Jessie thought maybe she understood something. The boy smelled like—was that alcohol? Not many men in Clifton drank—certainly not near any females—but Reverend Holloway waxed poetic on the evils associated with "likker." This boy might do anything. Or—he might be drunk enough Jessie could fool him. If she could just figure out what he was talking about.

"You thought I was a, uh, hitchhiker?" she asked, trying to make her voice sound as though it was a ridiculous idea. Whatever it was.

"Quit playing dumb," the boy snapped. "Tol and me don't want to wait. Oh—and we've all got to get to In-di-a-nap-po-lees."

He said the last part in a sticky-sweet voice. Jessie didn't move. The boy grabbed for her elbow. She jerked away. The momentum almost toppled the boy and he fell back against the car. Jessie couldn't help laughing.

The driver got out of the car. He had on a black T-shirt with his ripped jeans, and for a minute Jessie thought he might be the Megadeth boy from the Stopping Point. But his hair was long and stringy like his friend's, not cropped.

"Come on," he said smoothly. "Don't mind Ray. You should come with us before—before someone comes along who might hurt you. A little girl like you shouldn't be out hitchhiking. All sorts of dangerous people are out on the road. Get in the car and we'll protect you."

"Stop it, Tol. You're killing me!" Ray said, leaning on the car, laughing.

Tol circled the car toward Jessie. Jessie backed up. Tol didn't seem as drunk as Ray, but she couldn't be sure. Really, she couldn't be sure of anything. She'd never seen anybody actually drunk, except the pig when Andrew gave him too many rotten apples. And the pig was stupid enough beforehand.

"Now, Ray, you're scaring her," Tol said, giving Ray a mean look. Slowly, without seeming to, he took another step toward Jessie.

Jessie took another step back. In a minute, she'd be in the ditch, and the ditch here had water flowing in it. Her heart pounded. She might have been able to outrun Ray, but not Tol. Think, she told herself. You have to outsmart them.

Tol moved closer to Jessie. In a second, he'd be able to grab her.

"I'm not really going to Indianapolis," Jessie lied. "And I know where it is. I live over there in, uh, Waverly. I'm just taking a walk to—"

She paused, then remembered the fat environmentalist.

"I'm just taking a walk to lose weight."

Tol stopped.

"You're not fat," he said.

"Well—" Jessie watched him edge closer to her. "You leave me alone or I'll get my pa!"

"Pa?" By the car, Ray shrieked. "Pa? I haven't heard that since my little sister watched *Little House on the Prairie*."

"My pa's a big man," Jessie said. But her voice sounded uncertain even to her. What should she have called her father?

"Um—right," Tol said. "He'll be glad me and Ray are taking care of you."

His grin was too much. Jessie was so dazed by it that she

didn't see his final step. A second later, he wrapped his fingers around her wrist.

"Leave me alone!" Jessie screamed. She couldn't control her panic anymore. She yanked her arm away, turned, and ran.

She expected Tol to grab her again immediately. She was sure he was following her. Her wrist burned where he'd touched her.

"Help! Pa!" she screamed for effect. Then, because it felt good to call for Pa, even if she knew he couldn't hear her, she screamed again, "Pa! Pa!"

Still, no arms grabbed her. Jessie glanced over her shoulder. Ray and Tol were still standing by the car, watching her uncertainly. Maybe they did believe she lived in Waverly.

A fence separated the big road, 37, from the houses, and Jessie didn't want to slow down long enough to climb it. She turned by the green-yellow-red light and ran into a building that said KFC on the outside.

Shaking and panting, she paused just inside the door. She looked out the long wall of glass, but couldn't see Ray or Tol or their brown car anywhere. Had they left? Would they come back? Did they work for Miles Clifton?

"It's okay, it's okay," Jessie repeated to herself. "Oh, please, God, make it okay."

There was another door leading into the building, and Jessie finally pushed her way on in. She found herself in a large room full of tables and chairs and the tantalizing smell of cooked chicken. It was some sort of restaurant—Jessie had heard of such things, but she thought they were only in cities. Evidently she was wrong about something else. Once, she would have been fascinated—and hungry—but now she was too scared to care. She huddled against the wall for a long time before she got the nerve to walk over to a long silver counter. A woman about Ma's age stood there watching Jessie.

"Are you all right, honey?" the woman said.

Her sympathetic tone almost made Jessie cry. But she just shrugged. Maybe she couldn't trust this woman either.

"Is this Waverly?" Jessie asked.

"Yes," the woman said.

So Ray and Tol hadn't been lying about that. The disappointment hit Jessie like a wave.

"Is there a phone here?" she asked.

The woman pointed to a door opposite the one Jessie had used.

"Thanks," Jessie mumbled.

Jessie found the phone in a small entryway between doors. Her legs still shook, and she felt more like sobbing than talking. But she put her quarter into the opening at the top and punched the buttons like before, this time remembering the 1 first. Then, when asked, she put in more money.

The phone rang. Once. Twice.

And then there was a click.

"Hello?"

"Hello?" Jessie said, almost daring to hope. "Is this Mr. Neeley?"

"Yes. Who is this?"

SEVENTEEN

"Hello?" the voice on the other end said again. Jessie was too startled to speak, but all her fear and exhaustion melted. She even forgot Ray and Tol. The strange phone-thing had actually worked! She'd reached Mr. Neeley! Now, finally, she could get help for Katie and the others!

Then, because Jessie remembered how briefly everyone else had stayed on the phone, she began talking fast.

"My name's Jessie Keyser," she said. "I'm from Clifton—remember, you were against it? You were right about it being bad—now lots of children have diphtheria, and Mr. Clifton and his men won't get any medicine for them, and they're going to die if they don't get help."

"What?" Mr. Neeley asked.

Jessie repeated her explanation more slowly. It was strange talking into the clublike phone, but she reminded herself someone was listening. She finished with: "So will you help? Ma said you would. That's why she gave me your number——"

"What did your mother say I would do?" Mr. Neeley asked.

Jessie strained to remember.

"She said you'd call something—a stick—no, a board. A board of health? Then she said you'd call a news conference."

"Ah."

There was a pause, as though Mr. Neeley was thinking. Jessie was afraid he would say, "No, that won't work. There's nothing I can do." Jessie gulped. If Mr. Neeley didn't help, who would?

Then she heard, "Of course I'll help." The phone voice was crackly, but it couldn't have made Jessie happier.

"Oh, thank you!" she said.

"But this is atrocious," Mr. Neeley continued. "Simply atrocious, if you're right. Are you sure it's diphtheria? Are you sure there's no medicine?"

"That's what Ma said."

Another pause. "You're outside Clifton now?"

Jessie nodded, then remembered he couldn't see her.

"Yes. I've walked forever, because you didn't answer the first time I called, and then I couldn't find another phone——"

"Uh-huh. Who knows you escaped? That is—are you safe?"

"I don't know," Jessie said, remembering Ray and Tol. "There were two boys. . . ." She described what had happened. It didn't seem as scary now—as long as they didn't come back. "Do you think they work for Mr. Clifton?"

"Oh no," Mr. Neeley said, sounding surprised. "They couldn't."

"Are you sure?" Jessie asked.

"Yes." Mr. Neeley's voice was smooth again. "You'll have to take my word for it, because you're not used to things outside Clifton. They sound like ordinary hooligans. Has anyone else tried to stop you?"

Jessie didn't like it when adults told her she'd have to take their word for something. But this was Mr. Neeley, who was going to help. . . . She told him about the strange man who knocked her down at the Stopping Point, and about the camera back at Clifton that maybe caught a glimpse of her leaving.

"But no one captured me, so I guess none of Clifton's men know where I am," Jessie said.

"All right," Mr. Neeley said. "But I'm coming to pick you up immediately. Where are you?"

Jessie told him. "It's fifteen miles from Indianapolis. Get help for Katie and the others. That's more important."

Mr. Neeley laughed, almost merrily.

"I'll make a call or two before I come. And I can still be there in about a half hour," he said. "I take it you don't know how fast cars go."

"I've seen a lot of them," Jessie said defensively. "And I was in a truck."

"Oh," Mr. Neeley said. "Well. All right, then, now you'll get a chance to ride in a car, too. Look for a white-haired man in a black Cadillac—that's a big car. I'll be there as soon as I can. Good-bye."

The phone clicked and then Jessie heard a buzzing again, like when she'd first picked up the phone.

"Mr. Neeley?" Jessie asked. "Are you still there?"

No one answered. Jessie sighed. She'd never figure out these phones. But who cared? Jessie grinned as she put the phone back in its cradle. She'd reached Mr. Neeley! He was going to help!

But—Jessie's grin faded for a minute. Why hadn't Mr. Neeley asked her to describe herself? How was he so sure she'd be able to recognize him?

Jessie squinted, thinking hard, but after a minute she shrugged. She didn't see any other thirteen-year-old girls alone at the KFC. Probably Mr. Neeley knew that. She could go ahead and rejoice.

Jessie went back into the restaurant and celebrated by asking the woman at the counter for some chicken and potatoes and lemonade. It cost more than three dollars—an incredible sum—but Jessie didn't care.

"You look happier," the woman said, putting Jessie's food on a tray.

"Yes," Jessie said. "Everything's going to be okay."

She ate at one of the tables by a window, and divided her time between watching for Mr. Neeley and looking around at the other diners. She had barely finished her food when she saw a black car pull up outside the KFC. A white-haired man got out and looked around impatiently. He was tall and thin, and wore a white shirt. Though she knew it was probably silly, Jessie was relieved that he didn't have a cloth strip hanging from his neck like the strange man at the Stopping Point.

Jessie rushed for the door, then slowed down outside. She suddenly felt shy. Up close, Mr. Neeley had small, squinty eyes. But he smiled when she stepped up and asked, "Mr. Neeley?"

"You must be Jessie," he said, and walked around the car to open the door for her. "Get in—we can talk on the way to my place."

Jessie slid in onto seats that seemed to be made of leather. Mr. Neeley's car was even more luxurious than the Sewards' best carriage.

"Ready?" Mr. Neeley said as he got in the other side.

"Yes," Jessie said. "This car. It's so, so—nice."

"Thank you," Mr. Neeley said. "It's the newest model."

Jessie almost giggled at how polite they were being. It was especially strange when Jessie really felt like throwing her arms around Mr. Neeley and hugging him and yelling out, "Thank you, thank you, thank you for helping!"

"Did you call the board of health? And the news conference?" she asked eagerly as Mr. Neeley turned a key by the steering wheel.

"I did call the health department. But I don't think I'll have to call a news conference at all, because the people I talked to were going to take medicine to Clifton immediately. I'll just make a few follow-up calls later."

"Will my sister and the others be okay?" Jessie asked. Mr. Neeley winced, and Jessie decided maybe some people still thought "okay" was a bad word in the 1990s. She tried again: "Will they be all right?"

"Yes, yes. Trust me. I'm taking care of everything."

Jessie still felt a little worried—she probably would until she saw Katie and the others all healthy again. But she didn't want Mr. Neeley to think she didn't believe him. So she just nodded and sat silently as the car began to move. She heard a slight humming and felt a slight vibration under her feet, but it was nothing like the racket in the bread truck. Soon they were gliding on the big road, 37. It felt like they were hardly moving at all.

"How fast are we going?" Jessie asked.

"Fifty-five. That is—if we travel at this speed for a full hour, we'll have gone fifty-five miles."

Jessie gasped. It didn't seem possible. But then she thought of something—

"If we can go that fast, could you just take me back to Clifton?" Jessie asked. "I miss Ma and Pa, and I want to see Katie, and—"

It struck her as sad, suddenly, that Mr. Neeley didn't know Jessie's family. If Jessie mentioned Katie to any of her neighbors, they'd know exactly who she meant. But Mr. Neeley, as much as he was helping, had never met anyone Jessie knew.

"You want to go back to Clifton?" Mr. Neeley sounded shocked, maybe because he opposed the place. "I don't think that's a good idea. I didn't want to scare you, but Clifton's men could still make trouble for you. You're safe with me, though. I'll take you back when it's safe there, too."

"Oh," Jessie said weakly.

"Now, why don't you tell me how you escaped from Clifton?" Mr. Neeley said. "You were smart to find a way out."

"Ma did that, not me," Jessie said. She told him about the King of the Mountain rock. It reminded her how puzzled and worried Ma had been sending Jessie on her journey.

"There was one thing Ma couldn't figure out—can you tell me why Clifton became so dangerous?" Jessie asked. "Maybe I just don't understand tourist sites well enough. . . . Ma said

Clifton's men wanted everything to be authentic for the tourists—but I saw the tourists, and I don't think they wanted children to die. Mrs. Spurning, the guide, said modern medical care was available in Clifton, and no one got upset. Except me, because I knew it wasn't true—"

Jessie thought her question was getting confusing, so she looked at Mr. Neeley to see if he understood. His brow was crinkled. He looked—angry. But maybe Jessie just couldn't see very well because it was dark in the car.

Mr. Neeley was quiet for a long time, then he said, "That's a hard question. I can't answer it."

Jessie frowned, disappointed. Then she decided she shouldn't expect Mr. Neeley to solve everything.

In the silence between them, Mr. Neeley turned a knob near the steering wheel. Suddenly music surrounded Jessie. She jerked her head around looking for all the fiddles, flutes, trumpets, and drums.

Mr. Neeley laughed at her reaction.

"I take it this is your first exposure to radio," he said. "The radio—this box in my dashboard—picks up sound waves broadcast by radio stations. I change the channel to get different stations."

He turned another knob, and someone said, "—the weather tonight will be—" Another turn, and different music thrummed out, loud and raucous. Mr. Neeley switched back to the flowing fiddles.

The idea of a radio was so outlandish, Jessie almost thought Mr. Neeley was playing a prank on her.

"Actually," she said, "I guess I heard a radio once before."

"Really?" Mr. Neeley said. "Where?"

"In the bread truck." She described what she had heard, and decided maybe it had been a radio. Radio wasn't any more preposterous than the miracle lights she'd seen under Clifton, or the cars that moved without horses, or the strange cold that surrounded the bottles at the Stopping Point.

"Oh." Mr. Neeley paused. "And how did you get into this bread truck?"

Jessie explained.

"Everything outside Clifton must seem odd to you," Mr. Neeley said. "What was it like living there? Did you really believe you were living in 1840?"

"Yes, of course. Everyone did. Well, I guess not the grown-ups, but they acted like it."

Then Mr. Neeley asked a lot of questions about Clifton, even more than he'd asked about the diphtheria. At first, Jessie thought that was strange, but then she changed her mind. He knew what diphtheria was, but he'd never been to Clifton. So Jessie described the Keyser cabin, with the picture of Andrew Jackson on the wall. She described the school, where Mr. Smythe ruled with an iron fist—"or a big switch, whichever he feels more like using that day." She started talking about her family, Ma and Pa, Hannah, Andrew, Nathan, Bartholomew, and Katie. But a tide of homesickness overcame her, and she almost began crying right there in front of Mr. Neeley. This was the first time she'd been away from her family—and what a strange way to leave—but still, Jessie Keyser didn't cry in front of strangers.

"Did your ma tell your brothers and sisters what year it really is?" Mr. Neeley asked. "And do you think they've told the other children in the village?"

"Can we talk about this later?" Jessie asked, squeezing the words past the lump of tears in her throat.

Mr. Neeley looked over at her, and said in a kinder tone, "Sure. I forgot how tired you must be. When we get to my home, you can sleep, and I'll make some more calls, and then we'll talk about all this in the morning."

Jessie closed her eyes then, until she heard Mr. Neeley say, "This is Indianapolis."

She looked out at the biggest, brightest, most incredible place she'd ever seen. The lights, even outdoors, were so brilliant, Jessie couldn't see a single star because of the glow. And some of the buildings were swallowed in the clouds—"skyscrapers," Mr. Neeley explained, and Jessie remembered Ray using that word. Mr. Neeley pointed out the various landmarks—including the ornate state capitol—and Jessie gawked at the rows and rows of buildings. It looked like Indianapolis had done quite well for itself, after all. Several miles from what Mr. Neeley called the "downtown," there were still lots of houses and other buildings crammed in together.

It all made Jessie feel unbelievably small. But she couldn't stop looking around in awe. Even if just one person lived in every building—Jessie hadn't known there were so many people in the whole world.

Finally Mr. Neeley turned into an area where all the buildings looked alike, brown brick and tan wood.

"This is my apartment complex," he said, and then explained what an apartment was. "I live right there."

He pointed to a door that looked like every other door in the place. Jessie wondered how he could tell the difference.

But she thought it might be rude to ask. She followed him in the door, up some stairs, and through another door.

They entered a luxurious room with a floor covering that was plush and soft. Jessie had never seen anything like it. There were also huge sofas, soft and cream colored, big enough for two or three people to sit on at once. The sofas were even nicer than Dr. Fister's back in Clifton, and nothing at all like the Keysers' wooden chairs. After Jessie marveled over the sofas, Mr. Neeley showed her the TV, which was like a radio but showed pictures, too.

"That's unbelievable," Jessie said. "Are you *sure* it's not magic?"

Secretly, though, she was trying to figure out why Mr. Neeley's apartment didn't feel very friendly. It felt, Jessie thought, like no one really lived there.

"Do you live all by yourself?" Jessie asked.

"Yes," Mr. Neeley said, and Jessie decided that explained it. She'd never met anyone who lived alone. It seemed sad.

"This will be your bedroom," Mr. Neeley said, leading her through a wooden door into another room. "Here's your bed. Why don't you use the bathroom, and I'll get you a bedtime drink."

When Jessie came back from the bathroom down the hall—also incredibly luxurious—there was a glass on the table beside the bed.

"It's just water," Mr. Neeley said. "I'm not a doctor or anything, but I'm sure you're dehydrated after all that walking. You must drink this before you go to sleep."

And then he left her alone.

Jessie picked up the glass, wondering if the fat environmentalist she'd met was right about water being poison. This water looked perfectly ordinary, and Mr. Neeley seemed to think it was okay. But maybe nobody had told him. . . . Jessie decided it was safest not to drink it. She wasn't thirsty after all the lemonade back at the KFC, anyway. But if she left the water by the bed, she might forget and drink it when she woke up. She looked around for a place to pour it out, and finally settled on the window. She had to struggle with the latch, but eventually got it open and slowly let the water spill out. It splashed down two stories. Then Jessie put the glass back on the table by the bed and took off her boots and jacket. She felt bad that her pants were dirty from crawling through the ditch that morning, but Mr. Neeley hadn't given her any clothes to change into. She brushed the worst of the caked mud off the pant legs and lay down on the bed.

A few minutes later, she saw Mr. Neeley open the wooden door a crack and peek in. Jessie was too tired to talk anymore, so she pretended to be asleep until she heard him pull the door all the way shut.

And then Jessie thought she really would go to sleep, but for some reason she couldn't. She said quick bedtime prayers without getting up—"Thank you, God, for making everything okay"—but only felt more unsettled. She thought about all the times she'd been scared that day—leaving Clifton, meeting the fat environmentalist, talking to Ray and Tol. And she kept thinking about Katie and the other children, and how sick they were, and how terrible it would be if they didn't get medicine. Jessie reminded herself that Mr. Neeley had said, "Trust me. I'm taking care of everything." So why couldn't Jessie just relax and go to sleep?

To make herself feel better, Jessie crept over to the wooden door and listened closely. Distantly, she could hear the murmur of Mr. Neeley's voice. He'd said he was going to make more phone calls. Jessie decided to try to hear who he was calling, and what else he was doing to get help.

Jessie opened the door and slipped out into the hall. Mr. Neeley was in another room with the door shut. Jessie hesitated outside that door. She'd just listen for a minute, then she'd creep back to bed.

"Yes, I've got her here," she heard Mr. Neeley say. "I drugged her, so we've got some time. How much do you want me to find out? She knows too much—we may have to kill her."

EIGHTEEN

Jessie gasped out loud, then clapped her hand over her mouth to stifle the noise. What did he mean, "—we may have to kill her"? This was Mr. Neeley! Ma had said he would help!

"She doesn't suspect anything," Mr. Neeley was saying. "Remember, she's grown-up nineteenth century, not like suspicious teenagers today."

There was a pause, as if Mr. Neeley was listening to someone else. Jessie's knees quaked. She knew she should run—now!—before Mr. Neeley came out and discovered her. But she felt frozen.

"That doesn't matter," Mr. Neeley said, just on the other side of the door. "We started this, and we have to see it through." Pause. "No, we can't just take her back to Clifton. She knows too much. She's ridden in cars and all. I showed her a radio and TV myself. You think that doesn't change things?"

Silence again. Jessie's heart pounded. Her mind felt foggy and she realized she'd been holding her breath. She exhaled slowly.

"Of course I didn't *have* to show her the radio and TV, but I wanted to get her reaction, to make sure she'd never seen them before," Mr. Neeley said. He seemed to be listening again. "Well, we can all meet here. I can't leave the girl, and you're not leaving me out. Not now." Silence. "All right. Fifteen minutes. Bye."

So was he done on the phone? Was he coming out? Would he discover her listening? Then what would he do?

Jessie couldn't get her mind to believe Mr. Neeley wanted to kill her, but she managed to make her legs move again. She dashed back to the room where Mr. Neeley thought she was sleeping, and silently closed the door. Just in case he checked on her again, she lay back down on the bed and closed her eyes. It was all she could do to keep her body still and peaceful looking, when she felt so frantic. What was she going to do? What? What? What?

In spite of herself, Jessie's whole body began to shake with fear. She had to escape—but she couldn't get past Mr. Neeley. Think! she ordered herself. Could she wait until Mr. Neeley fell asleep? No—he'd said something about people meeting there in fifteen minutes.

Jessie tried to calm herself by repeating, "It's okay, it's okay," like she had before, but this time it didn't work. Nothing made sense. Why had Ma told her to go to Mr. Neeley if Mr. Neeley wanted her dead? How could Ma have been so wrong? Jessie didn't know what to think about Mr. Neeley, but she knew Ma wouldn't want Jessie to die. Was Ma even more confused about the world outside Clifton than she thought?

Dimly, Jessie heard the door into the apartment open and close. A man's low voice rumbled, but Jessie couldn't make out the words. If she listened, would she understand why Mr. Neeley wanted to kill her? Jessie crawled to the door to the main room and pressed her ear against the wood.

"Miles is panicking," she heard Mr. Neeley say. "Doesn't want blood on his hands."

"No—it's greed. He sees all that tourist money disappearing," a man's bearlike voice answered. "But he agreed from the beginning the tourists were just a cover. We have to remind him our research is more important than anything else."

Jessie couldn't hear the next response—it sounded like Mr. Neeley again.

Then a woman's high voice said, "Maybe we can have it both ways. We take care of the diphtheria deaths quietly and—bingo—Miles keeps his tourist money, we get our research."

More talk Jessie couldn't hear. Then, "No more tourists," the bear voice said. "Someone's bound to get suspicious if we keep running thousands of people through there."

Jessie remembered the guards back at Clifton talking about the village closing down. They had said there wouldn't be any more tourists. But why would anyone want to have Clifton Village without tourists? What "research" were Mr. Neeley and the others talking about? Why did they want anyone to die of diphtheria? Jessie's ear began to hurt from being pressed so hard against the door. She turned around, switching to her left ear just in time to hear the main door open and close again.

"Mr. Clifton!" three voices said, almost together.

The new person—was it Miles Clifton?—had a squeaky, panicky voice Jessie had trouble hearing. She heard him say, "—too soon—" and "you promised at least one generation before—" Then his voice soared: "This was a bad idea from the beginning. I knew it wasn't foolproof, if that girl could escape. We're all going to be caught—"

"Now, now." Mr. Neeley's voice was low and soothing. Jessie strained to hear. "—sensors picked her up the minute she lifted the manhole . . . decided to have her followed to see who she would contact—"

Jessie reeled back from the door. Had Clifton's men known all along she'd left Clifton? Could someone have followed her the whole way? She remembered the man knocking her down at the Stopping Point, and how he'd looked so deliberately at the note with Mr. Neeley's number. But how could Mr. Neeley be one of Clifton's men? She rubbed her forehead in confusion.

When she placed her ear to the door again, Mr. Neeley was saying, "—can't escape now. I gave her enough to knock her out for hours—"

Jessie could tell the next voice was Mr. Clifton's, but she couldn't make out his words. Then Mr. Neeley again, sounding huffy: "All right, all right. I'll double-check. I'll lock her in if it makes you feel better—"

Jessie scrambled away from the door. Mr. Neeley was coming—she had to get back to the bed! It seemed miles across the room. She was almost there—she could hear his steps outside—

At the edge of the bed, Jessie tripped over her own boots. She went sprawling, her head striking the bedside table. She hit the floor as the door opened.

Distantly, Jessie heard Mr. Neeley chuckle, "Well, well. Looks like our little time traveler fell out of bed."

Then everything went black.

NINETEEN

Jessie woke to pale sunlight on her face. Her head hurt, and she'd been having a horrifying dream about Ray and Tol and Mr. Neeley all chasing her in a rusty brown car. She kept trying to run away, but the car always pulled up beside her, with Mr. Neeley leaning out the window, laughing and screaming, "It's no use! We can go fifty-five miles in an hour!"

Jessie opened her eyes, glad to leave such a nightmare behind. She sat up stiffly. Disoriented, she looked around the sunny, unfamiliar room. Oh yes. She was at Mr. Neeley's. He had called to get help for Katie and the other sick children, and everything was going to be okay. He even laid her back on the bed after she fell—

Then she remembered. Mr. Neeley wanted to kill her.

Jessie shook her head, even though the motion made it

hurt worse. Surely that was a nightmare, too. But everything came back so vividly: overhearing Mr. Neeley on the phone, listening to the meeting with Mr. Clifton. . . . Jessie kept shaking her head. How could she tell what was true?

Her gaze fixed on the wooden door out to the rest of the apartment. Mr. Neeley had told Mr. Clifton he'd lock her in. If she'd dreamed the whole thing, the door would open.

Jessie walked unsteadily to the door. Her legs ached from all the walking the day before, and she felt stiff where the bread racks had hit her in the bread truck.

"I need someone to take care of me," she murmured to herself, wishing for Ma's best liniment and soothing touch. Maybe Mr. Neeley would give her something for her aches and pains, if only, if only—

The door was locked.

Jessie stood for a long time with her hand on the knob, absorbing everything the locked door meant. Mr. Neeley hadn't gotten help for Katie and the other sick children. He was one of Clifton's men, only concerned about some myste-rious "research." He'd tried to drug Jessie, then locked her in the room. He planned to kill her after she told him every-thing he wanted to know.

Jessie's knees gave out, and she slid to the floor. She remembered bragging to Ma—had it only been the night before last?—about how brave she was. Now Jessie knew she wasn't. It had been easy to pretend when all she faced was lit-tle old Crooked Creek or some silly half-trained horse. That "bravery"—bravado, really—had just been to impress the other Clifton children. Now she was in real danger, and all she wanted was for Ma to come hold her on her lap and stroke her hair, as though Jessie were still Katie's age. And, oh, Jessie had failed Katie and the others. . . .

"I'm sorry," Jessie muttered. "I'm so sorry." She huddled by the door. Maybe things would be different—maybe she could figure out how to escape, maybe she could get help from someone else—if only she didn't feel so muddleheaded and allover achy. But even her throat hurt. It took all Jessie's strength to keep from wailing like a little baby.

Outside, two robins chirped on the windowsill. Their cheery song seemed to mock Jessie.

"Oh, shut up," she whimpered.

The robins flew away. Then, seconds later, they were back, chirping again.

In spite of herself, Jessie raised her head and stared out the window at the robins. The window. Just because Mr. Neeley had locked the door, that didn't mean he'd locked the window. And it had opened the night before, when she poured out the water. She was two stories up, but maybe, maybe—

Stiffly, Jessie pulled herself to her feet and walked over to the window. The robins disappeared again. Jessie looked down. There was a bush far below. Even if she jumped into the bush, she'd probably break her legs. Especially since her legs felt half broken anyway. But wait—about five or six feet below her window, a brick ledge ran all the way around the building. If she could climb down to the ledge, maybe she could jump from there. Couldn't she?

Jessie debated. The ledge was only one brick wide. And it was awfully far down. What if she fell trying to get to the ledge?

She looked back at the locked door. What other choice did

she have? Was she going to stay here and wait for Mr. Neeley to come back and kill her? She had to try to climb out the window.

If only she could get the window open.

Hands shaking, Jessie fumbled with the window latch. At first, it seemed jammed, but it had been hard to open the night before, too. Jessie jerked on it with all her strength. "Please, please," she muttered.

And then, with a click that seemed much too loud, the latch gave way and the window slid open.

Jessie stopped for a moment, afraid that Mr. Neeley—wherever he was—might have heard the latch click. She listened for footsteps outside her room, but all she could hear were the stupid robins chirping out of sight and, more distantly, the sounds of lots of cars. She should go fast, though, no matter how terrible she felt. Any minute now, Mr. Neeley might decide to check on her again.

Jessie went back to the bed and sat down to pull on her muddy boots. Her hands shook so, she could barely tie the laces. How did she think she could climb down a wall?

Don't think things like that, she sternly told herself. You have to do it.

Jessie strapped her pack around her waist and stepped gingerly back to the window. It took her three tries to pull herself up onto the windowsill. Then she crouched, half in, half out, looking down.

"You have to," she whispered to herself. "For Katie. For the others. So Mr. Neeley doesn't kill you."

Awkwardly, she turned and eased her right leg down, feeling for the ledge with her toe. But she knew without looking that the ledge was much lower. She'd have to climb down and stretch both legs toward the ledge. She'd only be able to hold on with her fingers.

Jessie shifted positions, hesitating. Her left leg began to tremble under her weight. The longer she waited, the harder it would be. Still, she paused, almost in tears.

"I can't. God, help me," she breathed. Praying was better than crying. She hoped God really did exist outside Clifton. But what did she think He was going to do—pick her up and place her safely on the ground?

Then Jessie thought of pretending this was just another dare at home.

"Oh, Andrew, of course I'm not scared," she whispered, unconvincingly. But it was enough to get her to swing her left leg down.

"See?" she said.

She eased her body lower, lower, lower. And then her right foot struck the ledge. In a second, she was standing on it.

Jessie smiled. Even if she fell now, she probably wouldn't get hurt. Not too badly. The metal frame of the window cut into her hands, so she moved her right hand down, clutching the edge of a brick one row below. She moved her left hand down, too, and didn't fall.

"This is easy," she murmured to her pretend audience. "I could climb down the whole wall this way."

She moved her right hand down two rows, and the pack shifted against her waist. She lost her balance and started to fall. She grabbed wildly at empty air, then struck something with her left hand. The ledge. She held tight, and gripped the bricks with her right hand, too. Now she was hanging from the ledge.

Jessie grimaced over her shoulder at her pretend audience. "Okay, it's not easy. But it worked."

Jessie kicked out from the wall with her feet, and let go of the ledge. She landed in the bush, which was prickly and scratched her face and hands.

"Ouch," she said softly. "But—thank you, God."

Jessie looked back up at the window she had climbed out of. She half expected to see Mr. Neeley's face peering down. But there was only the curtain blowing out.

She'd escaped. She was safe!

Jessie sat up and hugged her knees. Tears came to her eyes again, but they were happy ones. She grinned, realizing she really hadn't thought she could escape. But she had.

TWENTY

Jessie struggled to stand up, and her grin faded. Her head throbbed and her legs ached worse than ever. She remembered how Mr. Neeley had told Mr. Clifton that "sensors" knew when Jessie left Clifton, and someone had followed her all the way to Waverly. What if Clifton's men were just letting her escape again to see where she would go?

Jessie thought about how the Keysers' cat, Abigail, always played with mice when she caught them. She'd bat a mouse around in her paws, then set it free. Just as the mouse began to scurry away, Abigail pounced again. By the end, the mouse was so battered and terrified, dying was probably a relief.

Jessie couldn't let that happen to her. She had to outsmart Clifton's men. But how? And she still had to find someone to help Katie and the other children. But who? Ma had said Mr. Neeley would call a board of health and a news conference.

Could Jessie call them herself? What were they? How could Jessie call them if she didn't have the number? And what if they turned out to be like Mr. Neeley—just pretending to help?

Jessie's mind felt scrambled with all the questions. Her legs trembled—maybe from climbing down the wall, maybe from being scared. There was too much she didn't know. She could hear cars zooming nearby, and the buildings around her loomed taller than trees. Indianapolis had made her feel small the night before, when she thought Mr. Neeley was on her side. Now that she was scared of him, too, what was she going to do? Whom could she trust?

It was all so confusing, Jessie felt like sitting down and bawling for her ma and pa, like a child even younger than Katie. Then she remembered something Pa said whenever Nathan or Bartholomew tried to eat a whole slice of bread in one gulp: "You bite off more than you can chew, 'course you're going to choke. One bite at a time. And that goes for thinking things, too, not just food."

So. What was the first thing Jessie needed to do? She glanced back at Mr. Neeley's building. As long as she stood right outside, he could easily find her when he discovered her missing. She had to get as far away as she could.

Slowly, because her legs hurt so much, Jessie began walking. She dodged behind buildings and turned as many corners as possible, so Mr. Neeley and anyone else looking for her would have a hard time following her path. At first, she thought she'd be trapped in Mr. Neeley's apartment complex forever, because all the buildings looked the same and she couldn't tell if she was getting anywhere or just going in circles, passing the same buildings over and over again. Then she reached a big street where the buildings were all different and cars zipped by in rows of six or eight. Could Jessie get one of them to stop and take her far away from Mr. Neeley? If she did, could she trust whoever stopped for her?

Jessie's legs shook more and more with each step. When she stumbled on a twig and half fell, half sat down, she decided to stay there. Just for a minute. The ground was hard as stone, but Jessie didn't care.

"You don't need to sit way over there," someone said. "I don't bite."

Startled, Jessie looked around for the source of the voice. She'd been too tired to notice before: An old woman sat on a bench in what looked to be a three-sided glass house, only about two feet away.

"Really," the old woman said, "you don't have to wait on the sidewalk. There's room in here. That's what the bus company built these for, you know."

Jessie stood up, because the woman seemed to expect her to. Cautiously, she went over and sat beside the woman.

"You don't normally ride this bus, do you?" the woman asked.

"No," Jessie said, hoping that was the right answer.

"I didn't think so. I tell you, the nine o'clock is always late. Always. That's why my daughter refuses to ride the bus. 'Not dependable,' she says. But I say, no car's that dependable either. Breaks down when you least expect it—"

Jessie saw that this woman was as big a talker as Mrs. Green back in Clifton. Everyone said Mrs. Green would talk to a stick if no one else was around. Jessie wondered how long she was supposed to sit listening.

"—oh, there it is. Almost on time, for once." The woman pointed up the street.

Jessie saw a big vehicle stopped about a half mile away, with people stepping in and out. The "bus" was kind of like the school vehicles Jessie had seen back at Clifton, the ones she'd thought were limousines.

"Well," the woman said. "Since you're not a regular, let me ask you this: Do you have exact fare? They'll give you change if they have to, but the drivers don't like it. . . . Say, aren't you a little young not to be in school right now?"

Jessie was saved from answering because the vehicle pulled alongside the three-sided house. The woman got up. Jessie wasn't sure what to do.

"Hurry," the woman said. "Tony's driving—he doesn't wait."

"Where's the, uh, bus go?" Jessie asked.

"Downtown, of course. They all go downtown, and you have to get a transfer to go anywhere else in the city. . . . Aren't you coming?"

Jessie hesitated. Could this bus be some sort of trap? Could Clifton's men have known she would walk to this intersection? Or could the bus be an easy way to get far away from Mr. Neeley's building?

Jessie's legs ached so much, she decided to take her chances. She followed the woman onto the bus.

"I'm Mrs. Tyndale, by the way," the woman said when Jessie settled into a seat beside her. "Would you believe I'm sixty-five? My daughter swears I don't look a day over forty, but you know how daughters can be—flattering you even when you know it's a lie. She's just jealous because lots of times, people think we're sisters. That's what she gets for spending all those hours out in the sun when she was a teenager, lathered in baby oil—"

Jessie listened only enough to be polite. She wanted to think about what she was going to do when she got downtown, but the bus was even noisier than the bread truck had been, and it made her head ache even worse than before. The bus sped forward and stopped, sped forward and stopped, over and over again. The jerky rocking motion made Jessie dizzy. She closed her eyes.

"You tired?" Mrs. Tyndale asked. "Bet you stayed up too late watching TV. That's what my grandkids always do—"

Jessie wished Mrs. Tyndale would be quiet. Then, even on the jerky, noisy bus, maybe Jessie could go to sleep. That was what she suddenly wanted more than anything else in the world. But no—Jessie forced her eyes open. She had to get help for Katie and the other sick children. Jessie might be out of danger, but the other children weren't. She looked Mrs. Tyndale over carefully, taking in the woman's frizzy white hair, her wrinkles, and her odd, stretchy-looking green pants and top. Could Mrs. Tyndale help? She didn't look like she knew anything about medicine, but maybe, maybe—

"Mrs. Tyndale?" Jessie said as politely as she could. Her throat was dry and raspy, and she realized she hadn't had anything to drink since the KFC restaurant the night before. She swallowed painfully. "Could you tell me how to find a phone number for someplace?"

Mrs. Tyndale looked puzzled.

"The phone number for what? Isn't it in the phone book? Or directory assistance?"

"What's that?"

Mrs. Tyndale frowned. "Don't they teach you kids anything in school nowadays?" She began to talk about dialing 0—or maybe another number that would be in the phone book or on a pay phone. Jessie didn't entirely understand, even though Mrs. Tyndale seemed to be recounting every single time she'd called directory assistance: "And one time when I was at the mall, I had to call my husband because he was late picking me up, and I couldn't remember his work number—it just fell straight out of my head—"

Jessie waited patiently for Mrs. Tyndale to finish. Outside the bus's windows, the buildings got even taller. Jessie realized the bus had reached downtown now, where almost all the buildings were skyscrapers. Many of the people who had packed the bus's seats and aisles were getting off. A knot of panic tightened in Jessie's stomach. How much longer would it be before Mrs. Tyndale left? And there was so much Jessie still didn't know. . . . Desperately, Jessie interrupted the old woman, even though she would have been spanked in Clifton for such behavior.

"Can you tell me what a news conference is?"

Mrs. Tyndale blinked. "Where did you grow up, child, not to know that?" Fortunately, she didn't wait for an answer. "It's kind of refreshing, though—most kids your age know more about that kind of stuff than my generation does—"

"So what is a news conference?" Jessie asked.

"Oh, you know, when someone has something they want

the whole world to know about, they'll call the media—all the newspapers and TV and radio stations—and they'll tell all of them to send their reporters to a certain place at a certain time so they can announce their big news all at once. And then the newspapers print the story and the TV and the radio broadcast it, so everyone knows—"

Jessie tried not to look as confused as she felt. How could such a news conference help Katie and the other children? Jessie couldn't think of a way to ask Mrs. Tyndale without telling her everything. Mrs. Tyndale did seem nice—but so had Mr. Neeley. Mrs. Tyndale chattered on. Heartsick, Jessie stopped listening. The bus turned a corner and pulled up in front of the state capitol. It had impressed Jessie the night before, but now she didn't care.

"Look, honey," Mrs. Tyndale said. "Over by the capitol. There's some politician holding a news conference, just like you were asking about. That's where I'd hold a news conference, too, if I had anything to announce—right there on the capitol steps. Then it'd show up real dramatic on the six o'clock news—"

Jessie looked where Mrs. Tyndale pointed. A man stood on the steps, and a group of other men and women clustered in front of him. Some in the group held strange-looking boxes on their shoulders, kind of like the cameras back in Clifton. Others seemed to be writing on their hands, or some bit of paper in their hands.

The strangeness of the sight scared Jessie, but she made a sudden decision. Nothing was going to make sense to her, so she'd just have to find a phone and do the best she could calling the board of health and the news conference.

"I'm getting off here," she told Mrs. Tyndale when the bus pulled to a stop.

"Well, it was nice talking to you, honey," Mrs. Tyndale said. "If you hold a news conference, let me know so I can watch it."

She chuckled as if she'd said something funny.

Jessie stepped off into a crowd. There seemed to be more people on that corner than in all of Clifton. And they were all pushing and shoving. Jessie almost lost the resolve she'd felt on the bus, but she turned to a young woman beside her.

"Please, ma'am, where's a phone?" Jessie asked.

The woman didn't answer.

"Where's a phone, please?" Jessie asked again, to anybody.

"I'd try up at the capitol," a man said, but he didn't even stop walking long enough for Jessie to say thank you.

Jessie shrugged and began pushing her way through the crowd, to climb the big stairs to the capitol building doors. The doors were heavy wood, more than three times as tall as Jessie. Inside, everything was big, too. There were shiny brass chandeliers, more stunning than anything Jessie had ever seen. The floor was marble, and huge statues lined the walls.

Jessie felt very, very small and scared.

The hallway was empty except for her and a woman in an official-looking uniform by a side door. She looked like the guards back at Clifton, so Jessie didn't go near her. Instead, Jessie walked the length of the hall and then up and down steps before she found a row of phones tucked away in a cubbyhole.

"Okay," Jessie whispered to herself, to build her nerve. "It's okay."

She decided to try the board of health first, because it at least sounded like it had something to do with medicine. Still, she hesitated. She reminded herself that she'd managed to call Mr. Neeley the night before. But she had had the number for him—and he had turned out to be evil. Did she have to use the phone?

Jessie thought about how Katie had looked up at her so trustingly, back at the schoolhouse. Katie—and Ma and all the sick children—were depending on Jessie. She had to try her hardest.

Trembling, Jessie pulled out a book labeled *Indianapolis Yellow Pages* from beneath one of the phones. Everything seemed to be in alphabetical order, with numbers alongside, but she couldn't find anything called "board of health." She remembered the thing Mrs. Tyndale had called "directory assistance." She dialed 0.

"Do you mean the city health department or the state one?" a voice on the phone said when Jessie explained what she wanted.

"State," Jessie said, with more confidence than she felt.

The voice gave a number and disappeared. Feeling a little better, Jessie dialed again.

"You have reached the Indiana State Board of Health. All lines are busy. Please hold."

"What do you mean?" Jessie asked. "Why don't you just talk to me? I'm from Clifton, see, and—"

"Hello?" a different voice said.

"Hello?" Jessie said uncertainly.

"Is anyone there?" the voice said.

Jessie decided she really did hate phones.

"Yes," she said. "I was trying to explain about the epidemic in Clifton. It's diphtheria, and Mr. Neeley said he was going to call you for help, but he didn't, and—"

"Excuse me," the voice said. "We're very busy. This is a child calling, isn't it? If there is an actual communicable disease report to be made, we will accept it only from a qualified physician. Good-bye."

"But—" Jessie said.

There wasn't an answer, just a buzz.

Jessie tried calling again.

"This is the same kid, isn't it?" the voice said when Jessie tried to explain. "Is this a prank call? We'll call the police if you don't stop."

Jessie hung up. Why wouldn't the woman listen to her? Tears blurred her vision. If she tried again, the woman would call the police. And maybe the police would tell Mr. Neeley, or take her back to Clifton. . . .

Jessie slumped to the floor beside the phones. The only possibility left was a news conference. But how could it help? Mr. Neeley had a radio and TV. What if the news conference just let him know where she was?

Jessie rested her aching head against the wall. Could she hold the news conference and then get on another bus before Mr. Neeley showed up? She felt too dizzy to make any plans. She wiped her tearstained face on her T-shirt sleeve.

"I'm too scared to do this," she whimpered. She closed her eyes. Unbidden, the image came to her of the night of Katie's birth. Jessie had only been seven then, but Ma had let Jessie help Mrs. Ruddle with the delivery. Pa said Jessie was too young for such a thing, but Ma said, "She's seen the horses and cows and cats plenty of times. It's no different." Only, it had been different. At the end, Jessie was left holding clean, tiny Katie, wrapped in a warm blanket. And Katie had reached up and grabbed Jessie's braid, almost like she knew her already. Since then, Jessie had always secretly considered Katie her favorite of all her brothers and sisters—she thought if the cabin burned down and she could only save one person, it would be Katie.

If she'd risk going into a burning house, she had to risk a news conference. She didn't know what else to do.

Unsteadily, Jessie pulled herself to her feet. Trying not to think what would happen if the news conference failed, too, she opened the Yellow Pages book and found a listing for newspapers. There were lists of TV and radio stations, too. Jessie painfully cleared her throat, preparing to make herself sound older. She planned a speech an adult might say. Then she dialed the first number.

"There will be a news conference on the steps of the capitol building in a half hour," Jessie said into the phone.

"About what?"

Jessie thought for a minute. She didn't want to give too much away now—

"Terrible problems at Clifton Village," she said. "And an evil man who's planning a murder."

TWENTY-ON

Jessie sat at the top of the tall steps to the capitol and rested her chin on her knees. She didn't know how long it would be before the news conference was supposed to start, because she didn't know what time she'd called all those newspapers, TV stations, and radio stations. She'd lost count of how many places she'd called—she'd used almost all her coins—but a couple of the newspapers had said, "We don't cover news conferences. We're just advertisers," and a couple of radio stations had said, "We don't do news. We've got an all-music format." Would anybody show up?

Maybe everybody had known she wasn't an adult. Maybe Jessie should figure out something else to try, to get help for Katie and the others. She didn't know what, though. Everything outside Clifton was too confusing.

Shivering despite the bright sunshine, Jessie reached into

her pack for the windbreaker jacket. But it wasn't there—she must have left it at Mr. Neeley's. She still had food in the pack, only a little mashed, and she hadn't eaten since the night before. But she wasn't hungry. The thought of hard bread or jerky made her throat close over. More than anything, she just wanted to close her eyes, go to sleep, and wake up safely tucked in her bed back in Clifton, with Ma hovering over her with hot soup and lemon tea for her sore throat.

Jessie closed her eyes, but opened them again quickly in case Mr. Neeley had somehow found out where she was because of all her phone calls. She didn't want him sneaking up on her. But instead of Mr. Neeley or Ma's familiar face, Jessie saw two men walking up the steps with the strange boxes—cameras?—she'd seen from the bus, at the politician's news conference.

So someone believed there was a real news conference!

The men paused a few steps below Jessie. Another man and a woman joined them.

"Hey, Joe," one of the cameramen said to the third man. "Know anything about this ten-thirty news conference?"

"Just that we got a mysterious message. It sounded like a prank call, but after that weird announcement from Clifton Village, my editor wanted me to check it out."

Jessie started. What weird announcement from Clifton Village?

Another woman joined the group.

"Who's holding this news conference?"

The others shrugged.

"Nobody knows," one of the men said. "I'm sure it's not the Clifton Village PR people."

"They wouldn't talk to you either, huh?" one of the women said.

"Just one quote, over and over: 'All the information we wish to divulge is in the fax.' It makes no sense—why close a multimillion-dollar tourist attraction for no reason?" the man asked.

"You don't believe the excuse of 'an unexpected need for maintenance and upkeep'?"

Another man snorted. "No. That's why I have better things to do right now than stand around waiting for a news conference that's never going to happen. I bet the Clifton Village people called this just to throw us off. If someone isn't here in five minutes, I'm leaving."

"Fine, Bob," a woman said. "You leave. We'll get the story. Doesn't the threat of murder intrigue you?"

Jessie sat still, trying to make sense of everything. Was Clifton Village being closed? Did that mean the children with diphtheria would get treatment that wasn't "authentic"? Or—did it mean some had died? Jessie felt more confused and scared than ever. The reporters' talk buzzed in her ears. Nobody paid any attention to her. What if they ignored her when she started talking?

"I thought some legislator might have uncovered a scandal about Clifton Village," a woman said. "But even legislators are never this late."

"Hey—maybe this mysterious source was murdered," the man called Bob said. "In that case, it's the police reporter's story, not mine."

"Nice attitude," one of the women said.

About a dozen people stood in front of Jessie. No one else

seemed to be coming. Still, Jessie didn't move. The reporters fidgeted.

"Ann, what do you think? Back to the station? We could go tape that woman who collects refrigerator magnets," one of the men with the cameras asked.

"Wait until Bob's five minutes are up," a woman said.

"It's one minute now," Bob growled. "Hey, kid. Seen any legislators—fat guys in suits—talking about a news conference?"

Startled because he actually seemed to be talking to her, Jessie stood up.

"I called the news conference," she said softly. The reporters stared for a minute, then began to turn away. Jessie felt like crying.

"See, it is a hoax," Joe said. "Just a kid's prank."

"You can get in trouble for this kind of thing," Bob said. "We're busy people. We can't go running all over town for nothing—"

"No, wait," Jessie said. "Please. You have to help. My sister and a bunch of other children are going to die if I don't get help, and Ma didn't tell me what else to do but call Mr. Neeley, and he didn't help. I heard him say he was going to kill me. And Ma said what he would do to help was call the board of health and a news conference, and I tried the board of health and that didn't work—"

The reporters turned back toward Jessie.

"Why don't you get this on camera, just in case," Ann said softly to one of the men with the strange boxes.

"Come on. It's just a kid," Joe said.

"We should at least hear what she has to say, don't you think?" someone else said.

"Slow down and tell us the whole story," another woman said gently. "Why don't you start by telling us your name."

"Jessie Keyser," Jessie said.

And then she told about the diphtheria, and how Ma had sent her out of Clifton to get help. She explained how Mr. Neeley had driven to Waverly and picked her up, and told her he was helping. Then she told how she'd overheard him on the phone and in the meeting with Mr. Clifton. She described her escape and the bus ride and her call to the board of health. When she finished, the reporters looked puzzled.

"Wasn't Isaac Neeley the crackpot who protested everything?" someone said. "Didn't he die—what, five, six years ago?"

"Yes, in a car accident. Would someone impersonate him?"

"Why? And why wouldn't they treat an epidemic? Clifton Village must be making a ton of money. What else do they want? What kind of research could they be doing?"

The reporters looked at Jessie like they expected her to answer the questions. She couldn't think of anything to say. The lights on the cameras blinded her.

"Isn't diphtheria kind of a nothing disease?" Joe said.

"Only because of modern medicine."

"I do think the girl believes she's telling the truth," someone whispered.

"Look, kid," Bob said, a bit more gently than before. "If this were true, it would be an incredible story. And we want to help you. But you can't substantiate any of your claims, or explain how this fits with Clifton Village closing down. We can't use vague allegations like this. Can't you tell us anything else?"

Sadly, Jessie shook her head.

"I don't even know why Ma thought a news conference would help."

"The idea," Ann said, "is that if lots of people know about the epidemic, Mr. Clifton and these other bad guys will be forced to let medical supplies in. If nobody knows about it, Mr. Clifton can get away with, well, murder."

"What is this—Journalistic Idealism 101?" Joe scoffed. "You know all you really care about is ratings. Isn't this sweeps week?"

Jessie looked from one reporter to another.

"Please," she said. "I know this all sounds strange. But can't you just take my word for it?"

The reporters whispered among themselves even more.

"What are you going to do?"

"I'll let my editor decide."

"But which way are you going to try to persuade him?"

"Wait," said the woman who had asked Jessie to tell her story. "At least we can prove if she is or isn't from Clifton. I was there not too long ago and watched the school—can you recite the presidents and the states, or something like that?"

"Of course," Jessie said. She closed her eyes, pretending it was just Mr. Smythe ordering her to recite. "George Washington. Elected in 1789 and served two terms. Father of our country . . ."

When she'd finished with the presidents, she moved on to the states. For the first time in her life, she was grateful to Mr. Smythe for drilling her and her classmates so much that the words came automatically. She felt so strange she couldn't really think.

"—Michigan, the twenty-sixth state, 1837," Jessie finished, and opened her eyes.

The reporters were staring at her. She realized she was beginning to weave. She tried to stand up straight, but it took too much effort. She collapsed on the steps. One of the women bent down and felt Jessie's forehead.

"She's on fire!"

Jessie closed her eyes, and the rest of the reporters' words seemed to come at her from a great distance.

"What should we do? Call an ambulance?"

"She's got to go to the hospital."

"I hope you got that fall on camera."

And the last thing she heard, before losing consciousness entirely: "Well, Bob, if that's diphtheria, you've got your proof."

TWENTY-TWO

For a long time after that, even when Jessie was awake, everything passed in a daze. She was vaguely aware of being in a bed, but she didn't know how she had gotten there. Soft hands tended her, sponged her forehead, and turned her on her side, but they weren't Ma's. At first, Jessie had trouble breathing, but then everything was easy. She would have felt totally peaceful, except, except—

"Katie?" she managed to croak once when she was being turned. "Katie okay?"

There was no answer. Jessie fell into troubled sleep and dreamed that Mr. Neeley and Ray and Tol were chasing her, brandishing giant phones the size of clubs. She woke up confused, but asked her question again.

"Katie okay?"

"Yes," a voice answered.

The next time Jessie woke, she remembered enough to ask more. "Others sick . . . Ma? Pa? Where—"

"Shh," a voice answered. "Just sleep."

And Jessie did sleep, for days and days, it seemed. She didn't know until later that her hospital room was filled with flowers from people who had read and heard about her—and even from some of the reporters who had been at her news conference. She didn't know until later that Katie was sleeping in a bed right next to her. She didn't know until later how many people were arrested partly because of what she said in her news conference.

But one morning, she woke up and felt almost clearheaded. She looked around the room and saw Katie grinning at her.

"Jessie?" Katie said. "Is that really you, Jessie?"

"Of course," Jessie said. "Come and see for yourself."

Katie shakily climbed out of her bed, wobbled toward Jessie, and crawled in with her.

"I thought you were in a box," Katie said.

"I was?" Jessie said, confused.

Katie nodded. "The nurse called it TV."

"Oh." Jessie suddenly understood. "That was—like a picture. Not real."

"But you moved," Katie said. "You fell down. I thought you were trapped. Then they wouldn't let me watch. They took the box away."

"Oh, Katie," Jessie said. "I'm okay now."

Katie started to cry anyway. "Where are Ma and Pa? No one will tell me." Katie leaned against Jessie and Jessie smoothed her hair.

"I'm sure Ma and Pa will come and get us as soon as they can," Jessie said. But she didn't know what Katie meant. Where were Ma and Pa? Why weren't they watching over Katie and Jessie?

"Who takes care of us?" Jessie asked.

"Nurses and doctors. They're nice," Katie said. "But I want Ma."

"I know." Jessie wasn't sure how much else she could ask without scaring Katie. "Have you seen anyone else?"

"Hannah and Andrew and Nathan and Bartholomew and almost everyone from school," Katie said.

So all the Clifton children were in the hospital. But where were the adults?

A few days later, when Jessie could stay awake longer, the nurses said she could see two more of her siblings. Jessie chose Hannah and Andrew.

They came into her room in strange chairs with wheels on the side. They looked odd without their usual Clifton clothes. Like Jessie and Katie, they both wore gowns that tied in the back.

"Look—I can do races in this," Andrew bragged, spinning his wheels quickly. But Jessie saw that after only a few spins he sat back in his chair exhausted. Did Jessie look as pale and sickly as her brother and sister?

"Do you know where Ma and Pa are?" Jessie asked.

Hannah and Andrew exchanged glances.

"No," Hannah said. "All we know is that this is really 1996, and there's something wrong with Clifton. No one will tell us anything else. They just ask us questions."

"Tell her the bad news, too," Andrew said gruffly.

Hannah nodded.

"Jessie—Abby and Jefferson died."

Jessie turned away. So she had failed to get help in time, after all. She blinked back tears.

Hannah rolled her chair beside Jessie's bed.

"Jessie? I know you went and got help and you saved all the rest of us, so you shouldn't feel too bad—"

"Oh, shut up," Andrew said roughly. He rolled his chair back. Jefferson had been one of Andrew's best friends, but Jessie knew Andrew wouldn't let his sisters see him cry. Andrew gulped and said in a forced voice, "Don't you want to hear what you missed? With the guns and sirens and all?"

It seemed that two days after Jessie got sick—"or you didn't really get sick then, did you?" Hannah said—Mr. Seward had suddenly rushed into the schoolhouse just before lunch.

"He had his big rifle, and he was waving it around saying no one would get hurt if we didn't move," Hannah said matter-of-factly.

Jessie was amazed at how calm she sounded, considering what a coward Hannah normally was.

"Why'd he do that?" Jessie asked.

"We didn't know then," Andrew said. "We thought he was crazy. But it was because of you."

Andrew and Hannah took a long time to explain, but eventually Jessie understood: After the news conference, all the reporters started calling Mr. Clifton and the board of health. Then the board of health called, demanding to be let in, and Mr. Clifton's men got desperate. Mr. Seward took over the schoolhouse, hoping to keep the health officials out.

"But why?" Jessie asked. "Why didn't they want the sick children to get medicine?"

"That's one of the things no one will tell us," Andrew said. "Now, shut up. We're almost to the good part."

Mr. Seward kept pointing his rifle at the children, Andrew said. Mr. Seward let Mr. Smythe leave, and the children thought he'd go for help. Instead, he came back with another gun.

"He was on the bad side all along," Andrew said.

Jessie was glad she'd never liked Mr. Smythe.

The schoolhouse was hot, but Mr. Seward wouldn't let anyone go out to the well for a drink. He didn't let them leave for anything.

"Not even the outhouse," Hannah said.

The children could hear shouting outside—voices they knew, like Mr. Wittingham's and Mr. Ruddle's, trying to convince Mr. Seward to give up. Then those voices stopped and there were others they didn't recognize, unnaturally loud.

" 'This is the Indiana State Police,' " Andrew imitated in a deep voice. " 'Come out immediately and you won't be harmed.' They had something called a bullhorn, Jessie. Do you know where I can get one?"

Jessie shook her head.

"Weren't you all scared?" she asked.

"Sure," Andrew said. "The girls cried. That's all you could hear—sniff, sniff, sniff."

"Not all of us cried," Hannah corrected. "And some boys did, too. The little ones."

"That's true," Andrew agreed, more charitable than usual.

From the shouting, and from peeking outside, the children could tell there were lots of men surrounding the school. They wore strange clothes none of the children had ever seen before: dark shirts and pants, with shiny helmets. Mr. Seward started sweating a lot, but he wouldn't answer the men outside. Then suddenly he rushed to one of the windows.

"Go away!" he screamed. "Or I'll shoot them all!"

He ducked back away from the window before they could shoot him. And that's when it happened.

"Tell her," Andrew said to Hannah. Jessie was surprised at the note of admiration in his voice. Andrew usually didn't have much use for Hannah.

Hannah looked down demurely.

"I tripped him."

Mr. Seward fell hard—"Because he's the fattest man in Clifton, you know," Andrew said. The rifle clattered across the floor. Mr. Seward lunged to grab it back. For a terrible moment, it seemed he would. Several of the biggest boys tried to reach it first, and it spun crazily on the floor. Then Chester Seward emerged with the rifle firm in his grasp.

"Good, son," Mr. Seward said. "Hand it over to Pa."

"No," Chester said. "You'll hurt Hannah."

He pointed the gun at Mr. Seward, forgetting Mr. Smythe had a gun, too. But Mr. Smythe took one look at Chester, dropped his rifle, and ran out of the school. The children could hear him yelling, "It wasn't me! It wasn't me!"

Holding the rifle at Mr. Seward's back, Chester walked him out of the school.

"That was the last time we saw Mr. Seward," Andrew said. "Or any of the other grown-ups. The ambulances came—you should have heard these things they have, sirens—and they brought all us children here. Even the ones who weren't sick. The nurses said we all had to be under observation."

Jessie was still amazed by an earlier part of the story.

"So Chester liked you after all?" she asked Hannah.

"Yes," Hannah said, smiling softly.

"Yu-uck," Andrew said.

"And you really tripped Mr. Seward?" Jessie couldn't believe it. "You were that brave?"

Hannah shook her head.

"No. I just kept thinking that you would have been brave enough to do it, and you weren't there, so . . ."

Jessie started laughing, hard.

"What's so funny?" Hannah sounded hurt.

"When I was leaving Clifton, I tried to be cautious like you!"

They all laughed. Hannah looked a little proud.

"So what was that like, your trip?" Andrew asked.

Jessie wanted to brag about her own bravery, but something stopped her.

"Scary," she said.

In fact, though she didn't tell Andrew and Hannah, she still felt scared even now.

TW NTY-THRE

That night Jessie couldn't sleep. The nurse turned out the light right after the supper trays were taken away. Katie said, "Night, night, Jessie," and almost instantly began the slow, even breathing of sleep. But Jessie lay awake, as wide-awake as she had been many nights back in Clifton when she went to bed hoping Ma would take her on one of her secret night missions.

This time, though, it wasn't thoughts of adventure that kept her awake. It was the horde of questions buzzing in her mind. Where were Ma and Pa and the other adults from Clifton? Why wouldn't anyone answer any questions? Why had Abby and Jefferson had to die?

Jessie tried to distract herself by listening to the sounds of the hospital: nurses conferring in the halls, carts with squeaky wheels rolling down the corridor, an occasional buzzing that Jessie thought might be a telephone. Jessie turned over. She turned over again. She still couldn't sleep. Why had Clifton's men wanted the diphtheria epidemic? How could anyone be that bad?

Jessie turned over a third time. She'd been in bed all day—all day for who knew how many days. She wasn't used to lying still so much. No wonder she couldn't stop thinking.

Jessie sat up, and felt a little better. Who said she had to stay in bed? Maybe if she got up and looked around the hospital, she'd feel even better. She'd be distracted, anyway.

Carefully, Jessie eased her legs out from under the blankets and over the side of the bed. She slipped to the floor, still holding on to the bed. Just the five steps to the door left her exhausted and dizzy. She was ready to turn back, but then she saw a wheelchair sitting empty a few feet up the hall. It seemed to be waiting for her. And anyhow—she'd return it when she was done.

Jessie sat down with relief, her legs trembling. At first, she couldn't get the chair to go anywhere, but then she figured out it had a lock on it. Once she jerked on the right lever and pushed the wheels, the chair rolled smoothly.

The hall, Jessie soon found, held little to distract her. It had a tile floor and dimmed lights a lot like the ones that had amazed her back at the tourist part of Clifton. But Jessie wasn't so easily awed now. Most of the doors along the hallway were closed. The open ones only revealed empty rooms with two beds and a few chairs—duplicates of Jessie's and Katie's room. Several nurses were clustered at a desk far down the hall, but no one else was in sight.

Then Jessie reached a glassed-in room with a sign, VISI-

TORS LOUNGE, on the door. It held lots of sofas and chairs. Jessie couldn't see anyone in any of the chairs, but she could hear voices coming from the room. One sounded strangely familiar.

"—for the greater good of science," the voice was saying. "There are always sacrifices involved in great scientific work. How many men were killed trying to fly before the Wright brothers succeeded? And how about Marie Curie?—remember, she essentially poisoned herself with radium."

"But all those were scientists who endangered themselves," said a second voice, this one unfamiliar. "Not defenseless children."

Cautiously, Jessie stood and peeked around the corner into the visitors lounge. She was glad now that the nurses were close enough to come if she screamed for help—if the voice belonged to the person she thought it belonged to. Of course, it couldn't be—

The visitors lounge was empty. But the voices went on. Finally Jessie looked up and saw a large box above her head. A TV. She understood now why Katie had been so upset seeing Jessie on TV. For there, as clearly as she'd ever seen him, was Mr. Neeley. And Jessie's knees trembled as much as if it were really him in front of her, ready to catch her again.

"Mr. Neeley?" Jessie squeaked, convinced he could see her as well. He kept talking, oblivious. Jessie sat down before her legs gave out. But she stayed by the door, because she couldn't believe she could be safe so close to Mr. Neeley.

Mr. Neeley disappeared from the screen and another man's face appeared.

"We're talking to Miles Clifton and Frank Lyle, two leaders of the Indiana diphtheria experiments," the man said. "Both are out on bail in connection with the case. Mr. Clifton has apologized to all involved. He's cooperating with the criminal investigation and says he wants to make restitution to the grieving families. Mr. Lyle still claims the experiment was scientifically valid and plans to sue the state of Indiana for interfering. Let's go to the phones. . . . Green Swamp, Alabama, hello."

Now the TV showed Mr. Neeley—was his real name Frank Lyle?—and a chubby, sweating man who Jessie guessed was Mr. Clifton. But the voice Jessie heard was a woman's, soft and drawling and angry.

"My question's for Mr. Lyle," the woman said. "Let's say, just for the sake of argument, that your so-called 'greater good of science' was more important than those poor kids. Just exactly what did you hope to prove?"

Mr. Neeley—for Jessie couldn't think of him with any other name—nodded eagerly, as if he'd been waiting for that question.

"It's not what we wanted to prove," he said, leaning forward. "It's what we wanted to save. Perhaps I should have said 'greater good of humanity' instead of 'science.' You see, with our modern medicine, more and more people survive diseases that humans used to die from. That's good—in the short term. But in the long term, the human race is weakened by all the weaker specimens surviving and passing on their weak genes. We wanted to create a strong gene pool that would endure even if the rest of humanity were wiped out—"

"And how likely is that?" the woman interrupted sarcastically.

"Much more than most people realize. Already we have supergerms developing that don't respond to our strongest antibiotics. Another generation or so, and we could be back to relying on our own immune systems. . . . Can't you see I wanted to save people, not kill them?" Mr. Neeley's voice became pleading.

Jessie couldn't understand much of what Mr. Neeley had said. What were antibiotics? What was a gene pool? Surely he didn't mean jeans like Jessie had worn on her trip to Indianapolis. But as confused as Mr. Neeley's speech made her, something about it reminded her of the fat environmentalist telling her that water was poison. Mr. Neeley, like the environmentalist, was sure that he was right. Jessie's stomach churned. Mr. Neeley couldn't be right, could he? Weren't Abby and Jefferson and all the other Clifton children—including Jessie herself—more important than whatever experiment he wanted to do?

On the TV screen, Mr. Neeley's face was replaced by Mr. Clifton's.

"That's what he and the others told me," Mr. Clifton said. "Can't you see why I was convinced? I'm not a scientist. I have no scientific training. I only wanted to help humanity by funding their work. They said the human race would be eternally indebted. . . . I'm so sorry. I never knew how they were running their experiment. I never thought about children dying—"

"Jessie Keyser!"

Jessie jumped so high she was surprised her body landed back on the chair. She turned around to find a nurse—the one who always woke her at night to take her temperature—glaring at her.

"Young lady, you do not have permission to be out of bed," the nurse said. "We have the entire hospital on alert looking for you. Don't you know we have better things to do?"

"Well, you can stop looking now," Jessie said. "I couldn't sleep, and then I found this TV—"

The nurse looked up at the TV screen and gasped. In one quick motion, she strode to the TV and flipped a switch. Mr. Clifton instantly faded into grayness.

"You are not to watch TV," the nurse snapped.

"But this is about Clifton. I want to find out everything that Ma couldn't tell me—"

"Oh no," the nurse said. "We have strict instructions. Believe me, this is for your own good. You've been very sick, and you aren't out of the woods yet. A severe shock could send you into a relapse."

"Then why do you go around barking my name and scaring me half to death?" Jessie muttered.

The nurse ignored her. "Back to bed. Now."

And the nurse made Jessie walk all the way back to her room, without the chair. Jessie was so worn-out when she reached her bed she couldn't even begin to puzzle out what Mr. Neeley and Mr. Clifton had meant on TV. All she could do was fall asleep.

TWENTY-FOUR

Katie and Andrew and Hannah and all the other children got better before Jessie—"because you walked fifteen miles and climbed buildings and held a news conference when you were deathly ill," one of the doctors told Jessie sternly.

But none of the children were sent home to Clifton with their parents. Instead, they went to places called foster homes. A woman known as a social worker came around and explained it to each of them.

"Your parents can't be trusted with you yet," she said over and over again. "The state has the responsibility of making sure they're good parents before you can go home."

"Of course Ma and Pa are good parents!" Jessie exclaimed when Hannah and Andrew told her what the social worker said.

"She says the diphtheria means they weren't," Hannah said. "She says Clifton wasn't a good place to raise us."

"That wasn't Ma and Pa's fault!" Jessie fumed. "And Ma sent me for help!"

But nobody listened to her.

Without the other children, Jessie was lonely in the hospital. The social worker visited once or twice, and a police officer came to interview her. But they were like the doctors and nurses—only asking questions, rarely answering any. The social worker wanted to know if Ma and Pa had ever spanked Jessie and her brothers and sisters. The police officer was interested in getting evidence about what he called "criminal conduct." Whenever Jessie tried to find out where her parents were or why the diphtheria epidemic had happened, the social worker and the police officer said, "It's not my place to explain that."

Whose place was it? Jessie sneaked down to the visitors lounge on another night, but someone had taken the TV away. She asked the nicest nurse—the one who always smiled even at the end of her shift—if she could see some newspapers with information about Clifton. But the nurse said, "Not just yet. Concentrate on getting better."

"I'd get better a lot faster if I knew about Ma and Pa," Jessie told her.

The nurse paused while turning Jessie's pillow.

"You're probably right. But it's not my place—"

"I know, I know," Jessie said. "I've heard that before."

The nurse soon left. Jessie lay in her bed and wished she could have another news conference. Only this one would be reversed: This time she would ask questions.

Suddenly Jessie sat up straight. It wasn't a bad idea—why not try?

Jessie slid out of bed and walked unsteadily to the ledge with the flowers people had sent her. She found the bunch of roses with the card that said, "The next time you have a news conference, I won't doubt you at all. Get well soon. Bob Haverford, *Indianapolis Gazette*."

Jessie called Bob from a pay phone down the hall when the nurses weren't looking. She didn't bother with anyone else. When she told him who she was, he greeted her like his best friend.

"Jessie! Don't you know every journalist in the world is willing to sell his firstborn to interview you? I thought maybe you'd hold out for big bucks from the *National Enquirer*."

"I don't want to be interviewed. I want someone to explain things to me." Jessie told him how nobody would answer questions, and how she'd been yelled at for trying to watch TV. Bob listened quietly.

"I don't blame you for being frustrated. I may be able to help. But my newspaper wouldn't be too happy about paying me to deliver the news just to one person. Let's make a deal—I'll answer your questions if I get to ask some, too."

"Okay," Jessie said.

The reporter arrived several hours later.

"I had to call in every single debt I had from every single hospital and state official I know," he said as he settled into a chair beside Jessie's bed. "I'm still not sure someone won't show up to try and kick me out. But I can be very persuasive. . . . Now, who gets to ask the first question?"

"I do," Jessie said. She paused, suddenly a little frightened.

Bob was a stranger, even though he had friendly blue eyes with his wiry beard and mustache. "Can I trust you?"

Bob laughed.

"I'm in a profession most people don't trust, and my ex-wives would probably tell you not to trust me as far as you could throw me. But I give you my word, for what it's worth, I'll tell you the truth as I know it."

"Okay." For some reason, that satisfied Jessie. "Where are my parents?"

"I don't know about your parents specifically, except that they weren't among those arrested. The officials say most of the Clifton adults are in custody for questioning, in hospitals under observation, or back in Clifton packing up."

"Oh. Why can't I see Ma and Pa?"

Bob shifted in his chair.

"You don't pull any punches, do you?" He tugged on his beard. "I think the state officials feel guilty that they didn't know about the danger in Clifton, so they're overcompensating now. They blame your parents—all the Clifton parents—for failing to get the medical care you needed. So they're not sure your parents can be trusted to take care of you now."

"But Ma sent me for help!" Jessie said.

"The officials don't necessarily see that as good. They think she should have gone herself, instead of putting you at risk."

Jessie scowled. "Didn't I tell you in the news conference? She couldn't fit in her modern clothes, and she would have stood out outside Clifton. She thought I could escape without being noticed."

"Do you mind if I write that down?" Bob asked. He pulled out a small pad of paper and began scribbling while he talked. "I'm not saying I agree with the state officials. I'm just saying that's what they believe. They're beginning to ask all sorts of questions, though, about whether the adults in Clifton were suffering mass delusion—like maybe they were free to go, but because they didn't think they were free, they're not responsible for their actions."

Jessie rubbed her forehead.

"That doesn't make sense."

"No," Bob said. "But as I tell my daughters, if life made sense, we'd all be bored. Want to see my daughters?"

He pulled out pictures like the ones Jessie had seen in the billfold from Ma. Jessie realized Bob was trying to calm her down. She smiled and nodded at the pictures of the three pretty blond girls, but asked her next question anyway.

"Why was there a diphtheria epidemic? Did the tourists want us to die?"

"Oh no, not at all," Bob said. "The tourism was just a cover—an excuse to get your families and all the others into Clifton and living like the 1800s. Then, too, it was a way to keep people from asking why they were building such a huge compound down there. The diphtheria was part of the experiment, not the tourist site."

"But that's what I really don't understand. What was the experiment? I heard Mr. Neeley say something on TV about a gene pool—what's that?"

"I'm not so great with science," Bob said. "But genes are what people inherit. A gene pool is—what characteristics are available to be inherited. Like if there are only blue-eyed people in the gene pool, no one's going to inherit brown eyes. So the Clifton plotters were trying to create a gene pool where all the people could resist diseases."

Bob explained that Mr. Clifton's scientist friends had planned all along to eventually close Clifton to tourists, introduce various diseases, and see who would survive. They had intended to wait until the first generation grew up.

"They planned to gradually remove your parents, so there would be no one like your mother around to know cures were possible," Bob said. "But the plotters got overeager. They stopped the modern medicine early—didn't you say at your news conference that the Clifton doctor stopped giving out pills that worked? Then at least one of the plotters introduced a diphtheria strain. After you escaped, they rushed to close Clifton Village entirely to the outside world. But that actually backfired—it just made the media suspicious enough to show up for your news conference. And you stopped their plot."

Jessie shivered, still thinking about the diphtheria.

"So Clifton's men did want all of us to die. Like Abby and Jefferson." She couldn't say their names without a quiver in her voice.

Bob shook his head.

"No—just the weaker ones. They wanted the stronger people to live. To create the strong gene pool."

The explanation scared Jessie. "So scientists think it's okay to—to let children die in an experiment?"

"No," Bob said. "Not at all. Other scientists are comparing this to the Nazi concentration camp experiments."

"The what?" Jessie asked. Would she ever understand anything?

"I forgot you wouldn't know about that. . . . Nazis were very bad people who ruled Germany—the country that you probably know as Prussia—about sixty years ago. They did terribly cruel things to other people in the name of science. And, like now, other scientists were horrified."

Jessie thought some more.

"What about Mr. Neeley—Frank Lyle, I mean? I know at the news conference someone said the real Mr. Neeley was dead, and I guess Clifton's men knew I escaped and found out who I was trying to call, but—"

Bob chuckled. "How did Frank Lyle fool you? Is that what you want to know?"

Jessie nodded.

"Yes. Ma gave me Mr. Neeley's number. How did Frank Lyle answer his phone?"

"Lyle broke into the home of the family who got that number after the real Neeley died. Fortunately for him—or for the family, maybe—the family was away on vacation. So all he had to do was wait for you to call. Then when you did, he simply took you back to an apartment he'd rented and pretended to be Isaac Neeley."

"Oh," Jessie said.

"As near as I can tell," Bob said, "Lyle was the ringleader of the whole thing, the one who convinced Miles Clifton to start Clifton Village. And I'd bet serious money he was the one who introduced the diphtheria early."

Bob stood up and stretched.

"That's an awful lot for you to absorb in one day. Isn't it my turn to ask questions yet?"

"Just one more question," Jessie said. "Can you tell the

state that Ma and Pa are good parents? And that Hannah and Andrew and Nathan and Bartholomew and Katie and I want to go home with them?"

"The state's not going to listen to me. But if I write a story about how a brave thirteen-year-old girl who risked her life for twenty sick children just wants to see her parents and go home—"

"I get it," Jessie said. "What do I have to say?"

"Whatever you really believe. Now, tell me—why do you want to go home so badly?"

Jessie told Bob everything she could. He finished up quickly, promised to come back to visit again, and left.

Two days later, a woman in a pink top and blue jeans knocked at Jessie's door. Jessie blinked, afraid she was just imagining what she wanted to see. But her imagination would have worn nineteenth-century clothes.

"Ma!"

Jessie started to jump up and hug her, then remembered she was still too sick to move so fast. It didn't matter. Ma was at her bed and already had her arms wrapped around Jessie's shoulders.

"Are you taking me home?" Jessie asked.

"Not yet, I'm afraid," Ma said. "Pa and I aren't going to be allowed to do anything but visit you for a while. But, oh, Jessie, it's so good to see you—"

Ma hugged her tighter.

"Ma, I didn't get help in time. Abby and Jefferson died," Jessie whispered.

Ma put her hand on Jessie's cheek.

"I know. It's a terrible shame—they shouldn't have died.

But you mustn't feel guilty. It's not your fault. And—you saved a lot of children who would have died if you hadn't gotten help. Now, how are you? Are you okay?"

They talked and talked until the social worker came in and said, "Time's up."

Afterward, Jessie was alone again. She stared out the window. She'd had all her questions answered, she'd gotten to see Ma, and she would see Pa the next day. Ma had comforted her about Abby and Jefferson.

So why did Jessie still feel confused?

TWENTY-FIVE

Jessie climbed to the top of the King of the Mountain rock and sat down, pulling her knees against her chest. She still didn't have her full strength back after the sickness, and her legs trembled a little from the exertion.

Around her, the cool, shadowed woods felt good after the thick August heat in Clifton. The trees were still green and leafy, but Jessie's sharp eyes could pick out brown patches, patches signaling autumn wasn't far away.

It had been almost four months since the night Ma crouched beside this rock to start Jessie on her quest for help. But it had been only a week since the state decided it was safe for Jessie and her brothers and sisters to live with their parents again. They'd all moved back to their cabin in Clifton only three days ago.

"Just like before," Katie had said brightly when the family all gathered around the supper table the first night.

"Yes, princess," Pa said, and smiled.

But Jessie knew things would never be the same as before. Abby and Jefferson were dead, and that still upset everyone. Besides, all the other families had moved away; the Keysers were allowed to stay only because Pa was taking care of Clifton while judges decided who should get the land.

Jessie bunched up her calico skirt in her hand. She looked like the old Jessie, "just like before," but that was just for today. Tomorrow she'd wear blue jeans and look like every other 1996 teenager.

For tomorrow, the Keyser children would all be going to a modern school outside Clifton. They'd ride one of those big yellow vehicles Jessie had seen all those months ago—she knew now that they were called school buses, not limousines. Jessie and the others would learn about all the twentieth-century things they'd missed all these years. They'd even do some of their work on something called a computer.

Jessie let go of the calico. All the others were excited about going to school and "being modern." Hannah had discovered makeup and marveled at how red she could make her lips and cheeks without pinching them. Andrew had fallen in love with cars and any other vehicle that didn't need a horse. All he could talk about was getting to ride a bus every day. He had the younger ones thrilled about that, too.

Jessie could understand why her brothers and sisters were eager to learn more about the outside world. But for once, she was the most frightened of the Keyser children. She wasn't sure she'd fit in at the modern school. And she couldn't understand why the others didn't see the difference in Ma and Pa: Ma, who cried sometimes when she thought no one was looking, and Pa, who had to be cajoled to wear modern clothes or talk about anything that happened after August 1840. Pa had to see someone called a psychiatrist for help.

"Jes-sie! Oh, Jessie!"

Jessie turned and saw Ma coming toward the rock.

"I thought you might be here," Ma said.

"I needed to think. . . . Did I forget some chore?"

"No." Ma looked up at Jessie carefully. "Things are pretty confusing, aren't they?"

Jessie nodded. "When I was little, I thought you and Pa knew everything, and you could protect me from everything. And now—" Jessie chose her words carefully. She didn't want to insult Ma. "Now it's not like that."

"I know," Ma said. "You went from feeling as safe as a five-year-old to finding out news that would destroy a lot of adults. That practically has destroyed a lot of adults."

Jessie remembered that the psychiatrist had said Pa might be trying to forget it was the twentieth century on purpose— because remembering would mean knowing he'd put his whole family in danger. The psychiatrist thought coming back to Clifton for a while might help Pa ease into the twentieth century. Jessie wasn't so sure.

"Ma, is everything going to be okay?" Jessie asked.

"I hope so. You have to remember—you may not feel safer now, but you are."

"But school's going to be different and—"

"Jessie, you coped with a lot when you went for help. I'm less worried about you than any of the other children. Or Pa." Ma looked down at her hands. She twisted her wedding ring on her finger. "I've got to go start supper," she finally said. "Stay here as long as you like. Hannah'll do your chores."

Jessie sat still for a while, watching Ma's retreating back. She thought about how scared she'd been, leaving Clifton that night almost four months ago. In spite of everything, she'd done all right on her journey. No—she'd done okay.

Jessie was still scared, but she felt better. She stood and jumped off the rock, letting the wind puff out her skirt. It was frightening, plunging through the empty air, but she believed she'd land safely.